SACRIFICED

PATRICIA BOYER-WEISMAN

This publication contains the opinions and ideas of its author. It is intended to provide helpful and informative material on the subjects addressed in the publication. The author and publisher specifically disclaim all responsibility for any liability, loss or risk, personal or otherwise, which is incurred as a consequence, directly or indirectly, of the use and application of any of the contents of this book.

WORKBOOK PRESS LLC
187 E Warm Springs Rd,
Suite B285, Las Vegas, NV 89119, USA

Website: https://workbookpress.com/
Hotline: 1-888-818-4856
Email: admin@workbookpress.com

Ordering Information:
Quantity sales. Special discounts are available on quantity purchases by corporations, associations, and others.
For details, contact the publisher at the address above.

ISBN-13:   978-1-954753-99-0 (Paperback Version)
                978-1-955459-00-6 (Digital Version)

REV. DATE: 16/04/2021

Acknowledgement

I would like to express my special thanks to my editor Gabriele M. McPeek who helped me in this book.

In her life, men taught her the different definitions of love.
Her father, the unhealthy, deviant type
Kenneth, casual sex
Saul, unconditional, parental love
Joseph, competitive love
Marcus, love for who she was
She grew into love and the hole in her heart was filled. Little girls should learn from
their first teacher, their father, a pure, healthy relationship.

Prologue

Samantha is a young but amazing lawyer who rose through the ranks, thanks to the influence of her adoptive father, Saul. Saul and Samantha had their first encounter during a guest lecture at Georgetown, where Saul was to speak on the influence of politics in urban development. He had noticed Samantha in the second row, and something about her struck him. This intrigue translated into a blossoming relationship as Saul quickly discovered that she was a misfit in that town. Samantha was able to fit in with the elites because of her intellect. Instead of exposing her as someone who didn't possess the right to mingle with the high and mighty, Saul changed her story. He gave her a law clerk as a mother and became her father. With this new identity from struggling rogue to the daughter of a high society man, it was no surprise that doors began to open around, and she quickly rose through the ranks in her law firm due to her sheer determination.

Samantha's love life is another chapter of its own. Her foray into relationships started with a man who she had a fling with. However, it resulted in a pregnancy neither of them was ready to nurture. Feeling violated, she got rid of the pregnancy and moved on wounded. While in law school, she became close to a man named Joseph, who carefully drew her close to him until he revealed that he had always loved her. Already crazy in love as well, Samantha and Joseph started a whirlwind romance that was filled with hot sex and a passion that never dimmed. Although his parents never supported the relationship as they had other plans for him, Joseph continued to meet up with Samantha as an act of defiance towards his parents. However, this romance ended in painful tears as he organized a getaway to give Samantha the worst news in her life.

Erroneously thinking that the getaway was only a prelude to a proposal from Joseph, Samantha was shocked when he announced to her that he had gotten another woman pregnant. Consumed by pain, she listened as he narrated how he slipped up with a lady who his parents had picked out from childhood as the one he would marry. He decided that he would have a low-key engagement with her to take care of the baby. Despite his insistence that it would only be a paper marriage, Samantha knew that their time together had come to a disastrous end.

Broken and dejected, Samantha was nursed back to life by her trusted assistant, Rick, and Marcus…the man who made her insides melt. Marcus was meant to be just a business client, but she couldn't resist the urge to penetrate through his calm exterior. Samantha seduced him after their meeting and spent a wild time between the sheets. Although she didn't know it early, her sheer dominance in bed and the control she exerted as she twisted his insides with pleasure had him hooked from the start.

There was something different about Marcus. Even though she still had strong feelings for Joseph, it was increasingly difficult to relegate Marcus to the back of her mind. It didn't help that he made a conscious effort to draw her closer. He showered her with attention until she couldn't deny it anymore and went into his arms. From there began another love story where the hot sex was never in short supply. It was a fantastic connection, and it would have gone well if things hadn't gone horribly wrong. Samantha never forgot about Joseph, and after a wild night in Marcus' arms, she couldn't resist the urge to call him again. Joseph wanted them to meet one more time, and she agreed. Marcus was making her feel uneasy, and all she wanted was to be with Joseph again. She would have gone through with it if she hadn't come down with severe flu symptoms that prompted her to visit the doctor. Shocked and distraught, she listened as she heard the dreaded sentence for the second time in her life…" you are pregnant." This puts her in a dilemma; WHAT HAPPENS NEXT?

Chapter One

Pregnant

Twelve weeks pregnant. That is about how long it has been since the Boca trip where Joseph broke my heart. That was about the same time I began to spiral out of control, back to all my destructive behaviors until Marcus rescued me. My head was spinning. Meanwhile, Marcus had filled my mind with healthy things – fun and talk, he even listened to my constant rants about all my troubles. One attribute that it is not precisely mannish these days, but nothing excites me more than that with him, there was no hint of pressure. He had successfully captivated my mind with all the essential characteristics of a healthy relationship. Suddenly, a sense of balance became clear in my life. There was no excessive drama. He was trustworthy and I could let lose my guard with him. He was responsive, and most of all, he was judgment-free. There seems to be a peaceful cloud hovering about him; he is that one person, after Saul of course, in this world that I can describe as my breath of fresh air. With him, I could be exactly who I am. He helped me know myself. He knew who he was and was willing to share that insight with me, in a type of friendship I had never known. There is no doubt about how sophisticated Marcus is; his choices are a delight, so are his words.

He lives in one of New York's platinum penthouses a few miles from Manhattan, typical for a rich man. He had mentioned he liked the penthouse; he did not have to travel miles to get to his office and it allowed for some alone time. Marcus's family owns a construction firm. He has a beautiful mind and body. He is smart, fun, and his family, unlike Joseph's, has no serial expectations of him that pushes him to make choices according to their demands. Marcus was free to make his own choices and he seems to have paved his own path. His love for the construction business is unparalleled. He has such creativity, and his broad, artistic mind has made him more successful in the business then anyone I know. When he opted to take over from his father's company, he brought his own unique ideas with him. Even though they made a fortune, he made sure to add a humanitarian flair to the business. He has a tremendous sense of family, which is clear in his participation in their affairs. He is a great big brother and loves his baby sisters dearly.

We were compatible in every aspect of our relationship, especially sexually. He was gentle at times and rough at other times. He knows my moods better than I do. He has already declared his love for me. It was clear from the day he entered my office, unannounced, that he was there for me. My wellbeing was his priority.

I continued to celebrate the awesomeness and goodness of a mere mortal man. He had brought so much joy to my world; it is so surreal. I was over the moon. I stole a sip of coffee I had managed to make that morning, after holding on to it for quite a while, it was no longer as hot as I wanted it. However, that did not stop a smile from spreading across my face. Marcus was supposed to be my prey, but it turns out, the spider was trapped in her very own web. I chuckled and playfully hit my leg on the footstool in front of my favorite grey sofa. Just like a sting from a scorpion, my brain worked itself through the momentary pain, reminding me I was pregnant with another man's baby. A man Marcus knew I still loved.

My thoughts went bitter, spontaneously, at the thought of not being with Marcus. I need to get all this out of my head. If I cannot be with one of the men I love so much, I know I have one in my tummy that I can nurture and love in some way. I need to talk to someone about all this, just talk. *I should call Saul,* I thought as I sank back into my chair, it was the most comfortable seat in my living space. I placed a call through to Saul and he did not pick up. *That was quite unusual,* I thought. However, just when I decided to call back, his call came in.

"Samantha darling, I missed… "

"Dad, I need to talk." I interrupted before he could complete his words.

"Samantha, come over at once. Bring with you an overnight bag for the weekend." He said with lot of concern in his voice. Knowing Saul, he knew something was wrong just from the intensity in my voice. He just knew it was not a conversation we could have over the phone. I always shared my feelings with him and he always knew what to say, or what not to say.

"I love you," he said as he hung up the phone. He could tell that my voice quivered whenever I was overwhelmed with decisions or problems and that I needed a sounding board. It was so great to have a loving parent. I admired that a lot about Saul and I hoped to be the same for my kids. I was troubled, and staying home one more minute meant that I was going to think about this pregnancy, and the men in my life, a thousand more times. So I threw myself in a casual floral jumpsuit, picked up the keys to my black Porsche, a gift I had gotten from Saul on my last birthday. The rims usually got me all toned up for a good day, but now, for the first time in like forever, my Porsche's shinny rims did not seem to have any effect.

I arrived at the mansion in almost no time. Saul's home was about 11 miles from mine and he lived in the downtown part of the city. The door flung open at once, like Saul knew when I would arrive, but the sound of my car on the drive was enough to announce that I was at home.

There he was, standing on the porch with open arms. I rushed into them trying not to cry, but the tears rolled from my eyes, which were already swollen due to the times I had wept and cried repeatedly. Saul just held me until I could pull myself together enough to follow him into the library. Sitting on the couch, still cuddled in his arms, he pulled out his handkerchief and handed it to me so I could wipe my face. The linen was monogrammed with his initials; he was a man of tradition. Well, that was until he met me, I had brought a lot of turmoil to his life, or so it seems. Instead, he saw it in a more alluring way, forbidding me to speak of anything close to it being a turmoil; his face saying that I had brought nothing but light and joy to him.

"Samantha Amanda Weinstein blow your nose and let us talk. You know you can tell your old dad anything." He said softly tending to my hair. I, for one, knew that when he called me by my full name, he was already on to me and just wanted whatever was troubling me out in the open.

"Dad…" I called out quietly, "you know, I never envisioned this. I made sure to use birth control, but obviously, it failed. You remember Dr. Rae's report, it said I'm in my 12th week." I did not even know if my words were making that much sense to him. In his arms I looked up and he spoke.

"Hmmm," still watching me the whole time. "Dad, I want my baby. I do not care what anyone thinks of me. We are in the twenty-first century, women have choices. And I've decided to have this baby." I said, sounding a bit more convincing.

"Samantha, I can't imagine you doing anything else. Why wouldn't you when you are successful all on your own? But always remember, you also have a father who loves you and there are the people who love you as well, like Rick and Scott. You have a circle of support and should know that we will stand by you and respect your decision. Life happens to everyone; it is the actions we take afterwards that decides the success of our decisions. Not every woman has the strengths or the support that you do. But you, my darling, will never be alone in whatever you choose." These words were a relief. He always had the right words to help me with whatever decisions I made. He was always there to rely on and his support gave me the courage to make choices that I wanted. He knew security in life was what I craved the most for myself. I released myself from his tender, soft arms deciding it was time to tell him the whole truth. I patted my belly gently with a dear smile across my face, knowing that Saul was watching me.

"So, you have chosen to make me a grandfather." He said with a smile on his face. He grabbed bottled water from the table and poured us both a glass. After having a sip, I felt less tensed. Saul furthered, "But, the only question is, are you going to tell Joseph? Do you think he has the right to know? In our circle, word gets out and the Joseph we know will want to be involved with the woman he loves. But life happened and he is married to another. To top that, he is expecting a child from that woman, who by law he is married to. It is only customary and ethical that every sane man acts responsibly and with honor. And we both know Joseph will honor your child as much as he does his wife's. That is who he is. Saul was right, life happens and I cannot hold on to what is not mine. He used to be, but is no longer.

Without hesitation, I retorted, "No, Dad, I do not want to tell him. I know that is being spiteful, but he made his choice, this baby will just make him feel obligated to me. If there is one thing I want the most, it is for him to want me because I am the love of his life and not because of the seed he has planted in me. I cannot play second to Emily. No, Dad, I cannot. I cannot play that mistress role while he pretends to be a devoted father and husband. I want love, Dad. So, I better not tell him." I said, grabbing a slice of apple from the abundant tray Maggie, the housekeeper, had placed before us. Again Saul gave me a *"hmmm"* coupled with a crunch of an apple slice. I looked out from the glass doors that surrounded the house to the flowers and butterflies finding their way through nectars and the breezy wind. My eyes almost teary, I continued, "I cannot have an abortion to make his life a little less complicated." My brain spiraled through the pain I had gone through while getting rid of Kenneth's baby, I could almost hear his voice when he said it was just a tumor. "I am not saying Joseph would have asked me to have an abortion, but I am aware his parents have expectations of him. They want him to pursue a political career, which is more of their own dreams than his, and I do not think I can fit into such a lifestyle. I cannot live my life by simply following another's orderly plan that leads to a goal that may not be the one he wants. My life is messy, but it's made me who I am." This time, I sounded a little more convinced about my own decision.

"So, Dad," I furthered, "we are going to have a baby." I said as I turned to face the only man I knew I could count on to be there through the entire process. "Margaret!" he called to a woman I did not know. "Would you please bring two glasses of champagne and a glass of milk? Come meet my daughter and let us toast to my grandchild, we are having a baby!" In walked a beautiful, well-poised black woman dressed in a fluffy gown. She was in her early sixties and her hair was grey and golden. She was carrying crystal glasses, one filled with milk and the other two with champagne. Looking up to her from where he sat, he said, "Margaret, my love, meet my darling, Samantha. My only daughter. She brings me more joy every day."

"Samantha, this is Margaret, the woman I have been seeing. I told you about her. She is the one I mentioned to you. The one that I was foolish enough to wait to declare my love for out of fear of what people would say." I stood up to hug her as I complimented, Margaret's hair.

"You are gorgeous." I spoke.

"Thanks, sweetheart, I'm pleased to finally meet you in person. Saul can barely keep your name out of any conversation." She said as we parted hugs and took a seat next to Saul. I sat at his right side smiling gently, forgetting my worries for a while and watching these old birds chirping at each other. He drew me in nearer saying, "Now, I have two heavenly ladies in my life." He seemed joyous. "My daughter," he furthered, "you've taught me that life is messy, but that is what makes it fun and exciting. And now, it is the right time for Margaret to move in with me at the mansion." Unquestionable is the love Margaret has for Saul and I was confident that she would love me the same. I had waited for this moment my entire life. Now I knew I had the mother figure I had longed for. I had a family and as unusual as it seemed, it was my family, warts and all. This pregnancy issue with Joseph would wait, tonight, we celebrate. Although I was overjoyed with how my dad was taking the news, anxiety, coupled with meeting Margaret, the thoughts of Marcus, and how he would receive the news seemed like a heavy stone in my mind. I would need to tell him soon. He would not take it well, that I know. But, not tonight, I am letting no one steal this joy. There is enough to be merry about. Margaret had prepared a delicious dinner and in six months or so I would have my baby. I was still wrapped in the cocoon of my father's love and smiling.

My weekend with Saul and Margaret was superb, and most of all, fun. I wondered how two old peeps could be so wrapped up in love. Indeed, the place of love is so beautiful. This is not to discredit Saul; he had done an excellent job as a dad, but having a complete family seemed to bring a whole new feeling to my life. We spent time talking about the baby and making plans. Saul declared that we needed to start at once on the nursery. Margaret made sure that weekend I was eating correctly and began to school me on raising children. She had three grown children of her own. She gave me a little insight into her relationship with Saul and how she had worked for him as a paralegal. Working late hours together she began to feel a connection to him that, over time, developed into an affair. She was married to a man at an incredibly youthful age, and even though he was a good man, she had outgrown him and began to want more intellectual stimulus. She loved Saul for how he accepted her for who she was but knew that if they went public with their relationship, it would kill his career plans to be a Supreme Court justice. A combo of a black woman and a white Jewish man would destroy his career. Saul was ambitious and had plans of making changes in laws that directly affected women, especially those of color, and she wanted these changes as much as she wanted to be with Saul. She also had two children to think about, and as time grew, she soon had a third child. Well, given the circumstances surrounding their relationship, after several years of working together and achieving important things, they were soon distanced from each other. Although at times Saul was ready to declare his love for her publicly, she decided to stick to being just friends, with no strings attached. However, he remained in touch with her, exchanging letters, bouquets, and little gifts every now and then to remind her of their deep connection.

"My husband always suspected that my heart belonged to another, but being a devoted man, he stood by me. He died a year ago." she said. My children are grown adults of their own. Eventually time, loneliness, and distance gave me the courage to call Saul and reconnect. He had been asking for me to move in with him, but it never felt right until now. My only concern would have been for my kids, but I'm certain that they will want me to be happy and will support me in my decision." She said as I smiled all along, listening to my new mom. I could tell from her story what kept them apart for so long. Saul had huge ambitions and would not let anything in the world get in the way of that. That gave me an insight into how Saul knew Joseph was not the right man for me, although he never entirely came out to say it. My father probably had more secrets to his life that he had not really shared with me. It made his wisdom seem more mystical somehow. That same weekend, Saul called all his friends, bragging to them that he would be a grandfather soon. He insisted that we began plans for the nursery and called his decorator, Mary, and had her bring over color swatches and catalogs on baby furniture. She assured him that she would have plans ready next week and get the nursery conversion underway. Saul wanted her to also include my apartment and a smaller nursery in my office so I could bring my baby to work with me. He called a friend whose daughter was pregnant and got the name of the agency that employed European nannies. He wanted the best for his grandchild. He wanted to throw a party so all his friends could be a part of the celebration of his first grandchild. He was bragging like he was the only person who had ever had a daughter who was pregnant with a grandchild. I just sat back and let him take the reins, it made him so happy. And I loved every minute of it. I was special and loved. He had his secretary prepare the list of names to send out invitations. He insisted I nap an hour each day. It was a weekend of love and care. I was so swept up in the planning and the excitement of expecting the arrival of my baby. No one mentioned anything about who the father was. In Saul's circle, there are no questions that might bring negativity to his joy, less you want to fall out of grace with him. He was a powerful man and no one wanted to lose his favor. I was wrapped in the cocoon of his influence and I enjoyed every bit of it. And even if I cannot have Joseph, I will have his child.

It had been twelve weeks, which means that I was three months pregnant. To think that I had eaten little in those three months got me worried the most. Well, not until Marcus intervened. I had had lots of liquor, too. It was only after he started caring for me that I began to care for myself. Memories of him brought chills to my spine, reminding me of how relaxed I seemed around him. I thought of the beautiful moments we had shared. I wished things were a lot different. Marcus was the man, but this is not his child. I was going to lose two of my most favorite men in my world. I was expecting a baby who will fill their space. I was consoled; I will not be alone. I was undoubtedly going to love my baby; *he is mine* I thought. The excitement of having a male child, whom I will shower with all the love and happiness I might not be able to get from a husband, filled me with hope. I giggled at the thought of a male child, but if it is a girl, I will love her all the same. First thing that Monday, I was going to make an appointment with my OBGYN to get a complete checkup. Delighted, I rubbed my stomach as I drank my milk. I was looking forward to the next six months.

***

With all its ecstasy and brightness, Monday arrived and I was scheduled to see Dr. McCullough at 10 o'clock. Saul and Margaret insisted on going with me. I had called Rick and told him I would be arriving late at the office. "Gotcha girl" he said, his favorite reply. Arriving at Dr. McCullough's and seeing all the hopeful mothers gave me an idea of what my body would look like at various stages of pregnancy. There was no wait; the nurse took me in at once and started with my weight and vitals.

"125 pounds and your vitals are good," she said.

Dr. McCullough had scheduled an ultra-sound, even though it might be too early to see anything, she could get a better idea of how far along I might be. She pulled my gown up and applied the cold gel to my stomach. Margaret and Saul decided to be in the room with me and I was glad to have their support. If there was ever going to be unwelcomed news, I wanted them by my side. She placed the monitor on my stomach and turned the screen and I could see a better view. There, on the screen, was a small beating heart and as she began outlining the details of the fetus, a puzzled look appeared on her face.

"Samantha, from what I can see, you are pregnant with twins. If you look carefully, behind the first fetus, is a second shape and another heartbeat. Samantha, you are pregnant with twins." She said, rubbing my shoulder slightly. I was thrown. Saul was gleaming with joy; he will be having two grandchildren at once. I was glad I could bring that much joy to his life. Margaret was not far away from being glad herself could see the joy of motherhood in her eyes, something I was about to experience myself. However, she was more concerned about my wellbeing, mentioning I had to gain more weight. Dr. McCullough had everything else checked and it seemed all was good. She told the nurse to give me a RhoGAM shot for my type B blood. She ordered more blood drawn for further testing and gave me prenatal vitamins and several books on what to expect during pregnancy, and a diet so I could gain the weight that will help my body sustain the pregnancy. "I will see you in a month." She said, seeing us out of her office.

We left the doctor's office and Saul's driver took us to a nearby restaurant for a late lunch. I sat there still dazed, while Saul and Margaret happily chatted away concerning plans for the babies. They both noticed I was quiet.

"Samantha," Dad called out. "We've got you." Margaret, in a very motherly like tone, said, "eat your vegetables, you are going to need to keep your strength up." I nodded in total consent. I was glad I have parents who cared and were on the lookout for me, despite the circumstances.

Thoughts of Joseph ran through my mind, how we made love without a care and how I just knew he was going to ask me to be his wife – well, so I thought. It is January and Dr. McCullough thinks I will be due to deliver later in June. But she did mention that twin children usually had a mind of their own and may come in earlier than expected. My thoughts kept on a voyage through different events, and it flashed to Marcus, the only other person who I had sex with before going to Boca, but only once. And then it struck me, could the babies be Marcus's? Could I be having his babies? We only had sex once, but I was on the shot. I was also on the shot with Joseph. Marcus had twins in his family, could it be...?

No, they must be Joseph's I thought making sure my mind did not tell on my face as I tried to eat my lunch. I looked up to Saul and Margaret and they just continued talking about the nursery and how to make my life a lot more convenient for their grandkids. Concerned that my face was giving me away, I returned to my thoughts. *Do I tell Saul? About, the first night with Marcus? No, not yet.* I concluded. I would tell Saul later, after I told Marcus.

Time had spiraled; it was already 2 p.m. when the driver got us back to the mansion. I had to get to work. As soon as the thought hit my mind, I rushed into my room and raced through the one thousand and one dresses I had in my wardrobe. Saul bought me so many new clothes every time he went shopping. It had always been like this, he knew my size, even my shoe size. I am lucky to have found me a king. I eventually found myself a black jumpsuit suitable for an office day and then before I could say *hey* my cell phone rang. Reluctantly, I picked up my phone and saw Marcus Matthew on the screen. He was the last person I would have thought to call. The last time I checked, he was away for some business in

Spain and we had not talked a lot since he left. We got to talking and he had managed to coax me into an early dinner around 5 p.m. since he just arrived from Spain. Immediately the call dropped; a hurricane hurriedly grew in my heart. I dreaded telling him I was with child – Joseph's child. How would I face him? How will he react? These questions and a hundred more throbbed through my mind, I just knew I had to brace myself for a disappointing night, but I had to tell him. I agreed he would pick me up at the office after work. I called Rick to tell him I was on my way. "Have Barbara double-check Mr. Smith's purchase contract and make sure the appointment is not canceled. I will be there in no time."

"Gotcha girl." Rick said about to end the call.

"Rick," I called out. "I have a surprise for you and the staff." I said, smiling gently.

"What would that be, please?" Rick said, trying to get me to tell him already.

"No," I said. "It can wait until I get there. See you in an hour."

Chapter Two

It took less than the usual time to get to the office and this was courtesy of how I fast I drove. The roads were less busy. It was after rush-hour and I raced through the traffic knowing that I had a client waiting for me in the office. I do not want to keep clients waiting. I got out of my car and headed inside my office. In a hasty manner I greeted Barbara, who was always at the front desk, with a smile and left for my office. Rick was patiently waiting on me with Mr. Smith's contract on my desk for review. He must have seen me exiting from my car outside the office building and decided he should wait for me in my office, knowing full well it would be the first thing I want to look at.

"Hey, Darling" I said entering the office. I was unmoved that I had found him inside my office, standing by the window starring at the world through the glass view.

"You should take it easy on the road, you know" Rick said sitting across from me with his hand on Mr. Smith's file. "You must have driven that poor girl at a lightning speed." He continued. I laughed slightly; it was casual of him. "Isn't that what it is made for?" I asked.

"Baby girl… you need to be careful on those wheels," he said. "Anyways, this is Mr. Smith's file." He spoke pushing the file over to me for my view. I skimmed through the document sparingly, making sure things were in order. I had intended to make a few adjustments to the contract to make certain of some issues. So, I took a note instructing Barbara to insert into the contract that in addition to buying the building, Mr. Smith would also be buying the air rights over the building for the same amount of money, that she was to amend the third paragraph spelling this condition in his contract.

Rick had made himself useful, seeing that I was busy with the contract and quickly made me a cup of tea. He returned once as I was done with writing and sat my Chai tea down on my desk. I extended the note to him asking him to send it to Barbara. He picked up the piece of paper and said, "Gotcha girl." He left the office to give the contract back to Barbara for revision. It was obvious to everyone precisely who ran the office. Rick was a super organized assistant and gives out assignments to each staff member. He would have been a good attorney but was content with running my office. He and Scott were like brothers to me. Together, they try to keep an eye on me. They both knew of my destructive mood and my past secret. My love for them is unparalleled. I had turned my chair around as soon as Rick left my office, sipping my cup of tea and stared out through the gigantic glass walls. Surprisingly, I was dead blank and could not pick on something palpable to think about which was understandable. I had done a lot of thinking over the weekend. I seemed to have accepted my thoughts and just as much, I have lived through so much already. Now, I wasn't alone, had Saul, Rick, Margaret, and Scott. I could hear footsteps behind me, I turned my chair around only to find Rick standing in my doorway. "Girl, you have an hour before Mr. Smith will join you in the conference room," he said. I looked up at him and wondered how much of me just a taker. My life was messy but they all loved me unconditionally anyway. I am a lucky girl and that had not always had that been the case. Saul changed that and had confirmed to me more than once that I brought more joy than anything to their lives.

"Rick, "I am pregnant." I spewed out. He clapped his hands to his mouth. "And before you say anything. It is twins." Rick was stunned, obviously perplexed at the news. Suddenly, he ran around my desk, embraced me in his arms, speaking in a whisper, "Ah! How did that happen, sweetie? I mean, I know, but I made your appointment for your depo shot."

"Well, Rick, there is a one percent failure rate, and I am the one percent. Be happy for me." I said squirreling out of his arms, leaving his embrace.

"Honey are you kidding, I am happy. You wait till Scott hears we are going to be uncles. We wanted children but neither of us wanted to raise the darlings full time. Saul must be turning cartwheels if the old fart can turn one. Scott will flip his wig," he said standing opposite me with a delightful smile. I looked at him knowing well that I got a good friend in Rick. He was always and forever supportive of me. "Saul is in love with the idea of being a grandfather. He already made so many plans. He wants me to have a nursery in the office so I can bring the babies. The storage closet will have to be cleaned out. In fact, he is out interviewing nannies. Saul wants the best for his grandkids."

"You know," I continued. "Saul finally brought Margaret home. They have been off and on for quite a long while, it is time they gave meaning to their relationship. Margaret is such a kind woman and we got along so well; she has agreed to move into the mansion." Rick had been aware of Margaret and Saul all along even before I had a clue. "That old bugger better make an honest woman out of her, she's waited long enough." Rick said, still staring at me curiously for more, he knew there was more to say and he wanted it all out in the open. I adjusted my chin slightly to show Rick I got the gist; we had few minutes before I will have to join Mr. Smith in the conference room.

"Quickly, let me tell you everything. I was at the OBGYN with Saul and Margaret, I had the necessary medical check-up, overall health is great, and yes, I need to gain some weight for the babies. They are due in the later part of June. Now, let me get ready for Mr. Smith. Kindly get me the revised contract." I said, checking myself once more to see if I was corporately dressed. Rick gave me another hug and said he would be right back. Barbara returned with the contract and I was looking over it once more. Rick joined me a few minutes later. He had left for the company cafeteria to get me a tuna sandwich and a glass of milk. He left me eating my sandwich and reading over the contract before Mr. Smith arrived. I took turns at the sandwich and cup of milk while I looked over the contract one last time. Rick must have thought about the babies and how much I need to add extra weight to sustain them. I concluded that the contract was good. I mean, "air right" could be the sticking point in the negation over the high rise. Without those air rights, the owners of the building next to him could sue to stop him from building a skyscraper of the height his plans had called for. I had already represented a small burlesque club called Monologue. The owner of an adjacent building had planned to sell the building next to hers and build a skyscraper. This would have cut off the view for the club. So, we just sold her air rights, paid off the club and the old historical burlesque club would continue with their performances.

When I entered the conference room, Mr. Smith was already seated with a copy of the revised contract in front of him. He was drinking a cup of coffee.

"Mr. Smith, thanks for your patience, I know my office rescheduled you while I took care of some personal business. And because you put your faith in my company, for that reason, I wanted to personally present you with your contract. I have revised your purchase contract. Paragraph three has been revised to include the air rights of the building. Air rights have become a source of contention in New York, so I find that spelling it out up front makes for a less clumsy negation."

He looked over the contract and read the paragraph. A broad smile formed on his face, replacing a confused one. "Well, I did some checking on your firm before I wrote that $100,000 check. Everyone said you were the best and I see from your thoroughness that you are." He spoke extending his hand across the table. I received it vehemently. "Thank you." I said. He flipped over to the signature page and signed it. "My bank has already been instructed to prepare a letter of credit for ten million and will be sent over to attach to this proposal."

Rick, of course, had great timing. He walked in with a glass of champagne knowing that it was time to toast to the agreement and the landing another million-dollar client. Our glasses were raised in the air, cheering to brighter and better deals. Mr. Smith commended us as he raised his own glass. I was glad we could close the deal and a few minutes later he took his copies and left. As soon as he left, Rick wanted me to come to the office cafeteria where he had the entire staff present. I had five attorneys, fifteen paralegals, eight researchers and five support staff. These employees were my work family. My office building had its own cafeteria which faced out into the hallway so that other offices in the building could use it too. Of course, Saul owned the building, but he let me incorporate humanitarian concepts into the construction of this space. The building had its own gym and a swimming pool on the upper floor. The idea was to keep people working longer because everything they might want to include in their workdays is just a few feet away. No one at the firm had any kids yet but there were always plans for a nursery when such time came. Rick had gathered everyone in the café,

"Samantha, we are here to congratulate you as the first of our working family to have a child. Everyone, raise your glass to our great leader, who's going to be the mother of twins."

There was clapping and resounding cheers. Rick interrupted the noise by inviting everyone to have cake and snacks. Angela stepped up to help serve the cake, which had a woman in a suit juggling a briefcase, law books, folders, a diaper bag pushing a carriage.

Yes, I thought, *that is me.*

As my staff gather around to wish me well, some of them had this puzzled look on their face. They must have been wondering who the father of my twins was. Luckily, they remained silent and none of them dared to ask. Nothing would be said to defame my reputation or the firm's. Working here was a privilege. My practice was considered one of the top legal firms in New York. We had people applying every day, we just simply did not have the space to hire more. Many of them were new graduates. We always had two to three interns working with us from the best law schools in New York. Rick came over and embraced me once again while I led the way back to my office, he simply just followed.

"You know, Scott and I are here for you, right?" He said as we walked side by side.

"I know you are. You're like brothers to me." I responded, having the last sip of my glass. "Rick, it's getting late, I should shower and dress. Marcus will be here at five to pick me up."

I hastily got off to my office, which was more like an apartment of its own. It had a bathroom, dressing room, a large closet and an inflatable sleeping couch. It also had a built-in bar area with a refrigerator and microwave. Saul had insisted that I add these to my office when he first did the build out. He knew with the hours I kept I would need this sort of arrangement sometimes. It had really been a promising idea, especially as unpredictable as my schedule could be.

The thought of Marcus arriving here ran through my mind, I had to prepare myself for the worse dinner date ever. *I am about to lose a man who is obviously crazy about me. I feel disgusting; however, a part of me just wants to see him and at least, kiss him one last time.* Marcus is one to keep to time and he will be here in a blink. It will be difficult for me to stand before that gorgeous man and tell him about my pregnancy. I thought about just keeping mute, the belly is not bulging. I might just as well enjoy the date and ignore his calls forever after this night. But Marcus was such a sweet man; he did not deserve to be treated horribly. He deserves to know. I can only hope that this does not come between our friendship and working relationship. It is almost certain that no man would agree to raise another man's child – not even Marcus. I soon began to change for the night, I selected a dress that flowed three quarters down my legs, there is no joy in being overly dressed and sexy tonight. I knew that Marcus would not want to go where another man had planted his seed, and I was carrying Joseph's baby, two in this case.

Chapter Three

I had decided to take the stairs, I needed to make myself do some exercise. I left my office condominium for the reception area on the ground floor. Using the stairs was an excellent way to get those thoughts out of my head for a minute. Only I could not help thinking, those random thoughts and speculations will not let me have peace. I have loved Joseph for a long time, but the thing is, I've never had a man who everyone around me loved, like Marcus. Although he is aware I was involved with Joseph, Joseph had no clue of Marcus, nor that we were seeing each other. I just wonder if he and Joseph, if they ever cross path, will get along. Obviously, Joseph knew he was the love of my life and got overly comfortable. He was just someone who could swoop down at any time, and I would be waiting. That was how it was for me, until Marcus. Marcus is a family guy. He has nothing to prove to anyone. He knows who he is and what he wants for his life. His family has not only made it easy to assume such a massive role in his father's construction company, but they have allowed him to find his way in life. He is a straight talker, confident, a little arrogant, organized, and he has a plan for his life. He wants to achieve those things that bring him happiness.

Marcus is a kind soul. He is understanding, non-judgmental, and he holds a strong belief that life was to be enjoyed. He said to me that he wanted a large family, kids crawling all over the place. He is a problem solver who would make a great dad. When he took the head role at his father's company, he worked to change its image. John Marcus Matthew Sr. had been ruthless in his business practice and had created ill will among his competitors, and sometimes his workers. Marcus changed that. He had fair dealings with his competitors; he made housing available to those who could not otherwise afford it, using housing grants and financing loans himself as the lender. He sponsored work programs for people who wanted to become a part of the skilled labor force. He developed a program for older workers, who had become displaced, to learn new skills. He went as far as making sure that anyone who was an immigrant had the correct papers and would help them get a job in construction in the United States. He would send me these people so that I could help them file their papers to become citizens. However, immigration was not my thing, so I often had to consult with an immigration attorney. Marcus raised salaries to a comfortable living wage, with benefits for his workers. He is a man of integrity, and lived it. He had zero tolerance for drugs, alcohol, or domestic violence among his workers.

He held his workers accountable, not only in their work-life, but in their home life as well. He had a psychologist on staff that helped his workers with problems. If Marcus fired you, it was because you simply did not see the same vision he did. He always had a waiting list for people who wanted to work for his company. He believed in education, as he was well educated himself, and he gave tuition reimbursement to those that wanted to further their education. He had even set up charitable organizations for women and children, but you had to be willing to work and better yourself if you signed on to one of his charities. Marcus believed in demanding work, setting goals, and reaching them. He also knew that finances were often related to family happiness.

Well, when you are a multi-billionaire, money goes a long way to make one happy. I loved all these traits and attributes he had. The Governor of New York often consulted with Marcus and they had become good friends. His life was not messy. Mine, on the other hand, had always been. All these thoughts floated around my head as I took the steps so slowly, as if I were being walked down the aisle for my wedding. But that was not meant for me, especially now that I was carrying another man's child. Well, married man's child, twins to make it worse. I had resolved that this was a blessing and a blessing it will be.

I was down the stairs when I heard the door to the reception room open. I had looked over at my Rolex, another gift from Saul, and noticed it was ten minutes before five. Marcus is a prompt man and he always arrived early. I took two snappy steps to the bottom of the stairs only to find Rick sitting on the reception couch. It was off working hours and the only person that should be left in the building would be security and Barbara. She seems to work late now that she has moved to an apartment closer to the office, she is indeed an extremely hard worker.

"Rick… you still here?" I called out, surprised he was still in the building. Well, he was the one person who would make sure I was safe, and tonight, he just wanted to make sure I was handed over to someone who would treat me with care. "Someone like me." he would say.

"Girl… you know better. I'm not leaving here till prince charming shows up." He said with an awkward twist of his head. He is more of a pendulum with his body language, swinging and swaying while expressing himself. "Come sit with me," he furthered, hoping that we would catch some girl time together. I continued to smile while I walked towards the fine fluffy three sitter couch in the reception room where Rick was seated comfortably. The idea of a couch like this in the reception room was to make sure that whenever our client's steps into the office, any ill- feelings they may have will go away and the warm atmosphere will make sure they are comfortable. And it has always worked – most of the time. Before I took a seat beside him, I hung the velvet cape in my hand on a coat rack just beside the couch; *it might get frigid out there tonight*, I thought while dressing up for the evening. I was about to sit beside him when the front door to the office opened. "Don't you share *my* lady with me, Mr. Rick." An alto voice spurred me to raise my head. It was Marcus and his voice was distinct. I did not bother to take a seat, because as he would, he had arrived on time – another handsomely, cultured trait of his. Marcus was dashing in a black, well fitted, heavy coat. He was one to radiate confidence by the way he walks, talks, and acts. He was so at ease.

"Not at all, sir," Rick responded, standing up with his hand outstretched. Marcus received his hand and they shook like gentlemen. "No really, I appreciate you taking care of this woman when I'm not around." Marcus blurted out.

"Pleasure is all mine," Rick said. They both stood there exchanging words for a minute while I gazed at Marcus' lips moving. I wanted him so badly, my thoughts were already on kissing those lips passionately. Rick decided it was time to leave us be and he wished us a pleasant evening. He went back to his office, leaving Marcus and I to ourselves.

"Ready to go, my sweet girl?" Marcus said, calling me back from my erotic thoughts. "It's pretty cold outside, do you have a heavy coat?" He asked. "I have the heat on and the car running. It's in front of the building so we can dash in." I picked my velvet cape and flung it on. In its pockets were my gloves and scarf, but I decided to keep my hands in my pockets. Marcus positioned his arm as if walking his queen down the aisle and I responded by tucking my arm in his. All at once, I felt an unusual sensation, journeying between my legs to my mind. It was a mixed feeling, one that made me think of our first night together and the other of telling Marcus about my pregnancy. I could tell he knew I was tense. He had left for Spain to handle business for quite a while, and instead of running into his arms like I obviously should have, I was aloof. I was only a couple of ticks and tocks away before I lost my friend, lover, and a charming prince.

"Yes, I think I have everything I need," I said, squeezing a smile.

"You look beautiful, my lady. I love you," he said, pulling me closer and engulfing me with a long passionate kiss. I instantly felt the heat of the passion; I wish he would grab my ass in his firm hands and send some strokes to my spine and tummy. I ached for his touch, but there is no going back about telling him of the babies.

With this situation, I might have to settle for days without his sexual pleasure, and the fun and adventure I had with him. I loved him, but in an entirely separate way. Our relationship is a good definition of comfort and safety. He is always there to clean up my mess without having to judge me, even though we are just partners. The thought of losing this man threw me in a state of panic; I wish I could change the narrative. A tear trickled down my face, but he was quick to wipe it off and ask me what was wrong.

"I know you have something on your mind you're not telling; we need to talk about it now." There was this conviction in his voice, he was certain I had something bothering me. I just held onto him, the warmth from his arms wrapped around me made for a feeling of just snuggling into his embrace, where I felt safe. "Marcus, can we get in the car and discuss it on our way to dinner, please," I said, still holding on to him. *This moment may not last forever*, I thought, *I might as well just enjoy what is left of our time together.*

"Of course, my darling, we will get through whatever it is that troubles you." He said compassionately. His Rolls Royce Phantom, a recent purchase, was sitting out at the front of the building, still running. The door attendant had left for the day, but the security guard opened the office door and locked it behind us. A warm and pleasant atmosphere welcomed us into the car. He got in after he had opened the door for me, stepped on the gas and zoomed off the highway toward Manhattan.

"My love, tell me what it is?" He spoke. Swinging his eyes from the road to my face. I could not help it. I began to sob. And through my tears, I managed, "Marcus, I am pregnant!" Pausing for a moment, trying to hold back the tears. "I am twelve weeks pregnant with Joseph's child – actually, with twins. Although I do not plan to tell him about them, I have resolved to raise them all by myself. However, the reason I am all tears is that I am not in the position to ask you to stay with me, because I fear I might have to let you go. I understand that you would not want to raise another man's baby, a man that I… love. I am so sorry, Marcus. I really could see us having a future together, with time. But I guess now I must concentrate on raising my babies."

For whatever reason, it seemed as if time had stopped since Marcus had hit the ignition. I had entirely lost track of life when suddenly Marcus pulled the car over.

"Marry me." He said, unexpectedly. I felt perplexed, but before I could mutter anything, he continued. "Even if they are Joseph's, I'd love them because they are a part of you. Moreover, they could be mine. You remember that our first sexual adventure was about three months ago – they could be mine. I have twins in my family; my mom was a twin." The firmness of his words gave way for an assurance, an assurance that felt as if that statement about twins in his family could be true.

"Remember our first night together," He furthered. "Our very first time we had sex, it was before you left with Joseph, so they could actually be mine. Samantha, even if they are Joseph's, they will be mine. Marry me," he said again, reaffirming every letter of it. "Let me give them my name. My family would support my decision if I am happy. I am happy, and I am at my best with you - marry me!" He kissed me hard on the lips, forcing my lips apart so he could explore my mouth with his tongue. He pulled me closer to him and caressed my back, running his hands ever so close to my bottom. Marcus never had to seduce me; the passion and fire I felt for him was insurmountable physically. I always felt like a wet towel, limp, and moist. I wanted him now, and if it had not been for this intense situation, I would have suggested we get in the backseat like two teenagers. That is how Marcus made me feel – young, adventurous, reckless, and yet safe. I knew whatever consequences that came out of our impulsive behavior, he was prepared to back it up with action. He was a man that lived life to experience the joy of it. He would not just take what he wanted but was prepared to accept the responsibility that came with his choices. Yet, he was selective in his choices, a virgin by no means, but I was the first woman that he had openly declared he wanted as his wife. He would fight for me; an experience no other man had even acknowledged. He had no lost loves, I was his first, and at thirty-two years old, he knew he wanted me to be his partner, his wife, his best friend, and the mother of his children. He flaunted societal norms with his macho swagger, and at an early age, his parents adjusted to the fact that this child of theirs marched to the beat of his own drum. That was copacetic with them. They knew he would make good, kind, and considerate choices when it came to women. His role model was his father, who married his mother late in life and adored her, and she, him. Obviously, he grew up in a blanket of love.

Marcus kept whispering in my ear, repeatedly whispering, "marry me." His whispers were only causing a romantic flair in my body; all I could think of was our very first night together. He had allowed me to have all of him to myself. He was not a weakling, but a man who is not scared to show how he feels and give to you humbly. Although I was in charge, I must say he is well- endowed. He was almost too big for me to take him fully into my mouth. At a point, he was letting out soft moans, and I was lost in the euphoria letting all hell break loose while I rode on his cock like I was on a horse. I lost time when I came, only to find myself wet again. He had so much endurance, the euphoria never ended. A man like him would have preferred being in charge than being submissive, which is quite reasonable for a rich kid who could get whoever he wanted, whatever he wanted, whenever he wanted it. Mike and Elton had confided that he had left a trail of broken hearts. But not with me, I am what he wants, problems and all. Only Marcus loved me enough to ask me to marry him with the uncertainty of whoever the real father was. The first night we were together, he laid vulnerable while cuffed to the bed. It spoke a lot about his confidence and self-esteem, he was not a wimp, but he was willing to amend the rules just to accommodate me. All this only caused more drips in between my legs as he continued to whisper, "marry me." I stared at him, and those moments flashed through my very own eyes like moving through a trance. I soon snapped out of it, "How can I think when you've gotten me so stirred up sexually?" I said, pushing him back. He had this mischievous grin on his face, "I knew that I wanted you for my wife the first dinner I had with you."

"But Marcus, if they are Joseph's, you may change your mind. You may grow to resent them because they will be a part of him." I spoke.

"So, if they are Joseph's, aren't they still a part of you? You play the key role in their being, Joseph had a few moments of pleasure, and besides, it is the man who raises them that becomes their father, not who sires them." Whatever it was he said, set my thoughts on Saul. I love him so much, even though he is not my biological dad. He loves me unconditionally, and though he came into my life at a later stage, we fell in love as a daughter and father instantly. Whereas, with my biological father, I detest and have nothing but disgust for him. Then there was Margaret, I had just met her and already I felt her motherly concern for me. And Kenneth – I do not even want to think of him, but what a disaster he would have been as a father. Joseph, I did not know what sort of parent he would be, but I certainly know him well enough to think that career would come first, not family. He had a lot of maturing to do to get his properties straight, especially where I was concerned. This whole child discussion never ensued between us, but I assumed he wanted children. When he found out Emily was pregnant with his child, he did what he thought was right. Marcus had openly talked about how he wanted a house full of children. Marcus would be a good father, no matter the circumstances of the child's birth. I continued watching him in between tears and happiness. He said, "I will never change my mind," reaching into his coat pocket as if wanting to pull out a hanky to help with my teary eyes, only to see in his hand, a triangle blue box.

My hands were at my mouth; *I cannot believe it,* I thought, *how can I be blessed with so much? Even with all the mess?* I decided it was best I keep calm and see this through; it might as well be a necklace. He opened it and inside was a five carat, flawless diamond ring set in platinum. "You see, Samantha, I came prepared tonight to ask you to be my wife without even knowing about the babies." He took my silence for a yes. He took my finger and slid on the ring. It fit perfectly, and the sparkle of the diamond was blinding.

"Not even telling me about Joseph being the love of your life or about your babies will deter me. I love you. You are my soul mate, my first and only love." He placed my hand underneath his coat and said, "nothing we ever do will be ordinary or boring. I love you, and life might be challenging, mystical, and yes, messy, but it will be our life. We will fashion it the way we want it. So, say yes, and make me the happiest man in the world." I just sat there, perplexed. Seeing that I was still stunned, Marcus suggested that we go over to the restaurant for dinner. He got back on the road and headed to our favorite Italian restaurant. My eyes switched focus and I was looking down at my beautiful ring. I heard myself whisper *yes* solemnly. He smiled and pulled into the restaurant parking lot, which was empty, quite unusual at this time of the night. But well, it is our night and the heavens might be smiling on my little ass.

As we entered the restaurant host met us in the lobby and said, "This way, Mr. Matthew, we have your table ready." I entered a restaurant that had no one in it and, in the center of the main dining room, was the most beautifully set table. It had tiny orchids sprinkled across the linen tablecloth, candles were lit, and a three-piece band was playing music.

"Elizabeth," Marcus asked, "will you take Samantha's cloak, please?" As he pulled out my chair, I asked. "Marcus, did you book the entire restaurant?"

"Yes, I had all this arranged before you told me about the babies."

Maximilian came out to greet us, saying, "Mr. Matthew, we are so pleased to have you tonight, can we get you and your Misses a glass of champagne before I send out the first course?"

"Max, my friend, I have some exciting news." He took my hand in his, the hand with the ring he had earlier put on and said, "Max, the good news is that Samantha has agreed to be my wife, and soon, I'm going to be a father of twins."

With a broad smile on his face, Max replied, "Congratulations, Mr. Matthew. I have six blessed children myself. I understand you must be so delighted." He shook Marcus's hand and planted kisses me on both sides of my cheek. "How beautiful," he said.

"So… Champagne?" Mr. Matthew.

"Milk…. Max, milk will be fine… we have a baby now remember?" Marcus said, smiling tenderly at me. I thought about it all for a minute and realized how shocking and unrealistic it may sound that no one questions Marcus Matthew. Max took his leave and left the table to attend to our dinner request.

"Darling, I think it's best I call your father and officially ask for your hand."

"That will make Saul incredibly happy. Thank You." I replied.

"Samantha, I promise you, you will want for nothing. And I understand you may not love me that much, but it will grow. If there is one thing you should be certain of, it will be that I will be a devoted husband and father."

"Marcus, I do love you. A whole lot, from my heart of hearts. Things are a lot different with you, more comforting and less conflicting for me. You are one of a kind, and …yes, yes, yes, yes. I want to be the first person you see in the morning and the last person before you sleep at night. I will be blessed to be your wife, Marcus – blessed!"

Chapter 4

The Proposal

Marcus dipped his hand in the inner pocket of his black two-buttoned suede suit and reached for his phone. He was a man with a craving for black suits and he looked dashing in them. I could just grab him and have him raw at this moment, as far as I was concerned. We were the only ones here in the restaurants anyway. I kept my gaze on him, trying to keep my lips wet and my imaginations to myself.

Saul's phone started ringing as Marcus placed the call on loudspeaker and placed it on our table. "Hey Marcus, how are you doing tonight?" Saul hummed over the phone.

"Hello sir, I hope it's not too late to have a talk with you?"

"Yes, Marcus, please. It's a young night; I'm here with my beautiful Margaret sipping some old admiral brandy." Saul replied, sounding well awake. *Typical,* I said to myself. Saul was never the type to leave for bed earlier than 2 a.m. and still he will be up and going at 6 a.m. the next morning. This was the routine he was accustomed to since his days at the Supreme Court, and retiring was the last thing that would take that away from him.

"Oh, alright sir." Marcus replied, staring deeply into my eyes, "thing is... I would like to ask for your daughters' hand in marriage," he furthered. "I know how precious she is and I promise to take loving care of her, be a faithful husband, and a good and attentive father. I plan to give you many grandchildren, and if your gorgeous daughter will be mine to keep, and you will give your blessings, I promise to give your name to one of your grandkids."

"Interesting, Marcus, that's pretty persuasive. But, well, are you properly informed of the baggage that comes with this? More so, as much as you have managed to win me over firsthand with grandkids, I still think that I did not hear that you love my daughter enough, you never mentioned anything close to love." At that moment, Marcus took my hand and replied, "Sir, I love and will continue to love her with my life, enough for her to carry that love long after I die. She will not have to ever want for anything, I love her enough to let her go if she ever wishes to leave me."

"Well, Marcus, my boy, I'll be honored to have you as a son-in-law. However, I am aware that you are Catholic, and if you would not consider this too much of a request, I wish that the kids of your marriage be raised in the Jewish way as well, so when they grow up, they understand that there are different beliefs and customs that they may want to carry on." Saul said, pausing for a few seconds, "You know, Samantha is my only child, and I would miss seeing her, but if you would grant my request, I'll be comforted." He furthered.

"Sir, that won't be a problem. I will have them trained in the Jewish faith as much as the Catholic faith. I enjoy Sunday dinners and beating you at the game of chess, so, we will always be around. You just may have lots of grandchildren crawling around. I wish a house full of kids and so does Samantha."

"Well, this is where I hear from the horse's mouth" Saul said, calling out my name, "Samantha," he must have heard my voice well enough to know I would have been listening to the conversations all along. "Are you sure you want to spend the rest of your life with Marcus?"

"Yes dad, I do." I said, blushing at the phone. "I find peace and comfort with Marcus. I do love him, dad." Before I could say anything more, Saul chipped in again, "Samantha, he is Catholic and will want a Catholic wedding." Just as if he had known my reply, he already started talking of a wedding ceremony. He obviously knows how I feel for Marcus.

"Dad, don't worry yourself. I plan to combine our faith's during the wedding."

"Well, my daughter, the checkbook is open and the checks are blank; just tell me who to pay." He said with some sort of sweetness.

"Dad, I'll be asking Rick to plan and organize the wedding. I am just going to tell him what I want. But Dad, I am scared for your checkbook, because I really want a splashy social weeding." Saul and Margaret broke out in laughter. "I think Samantha is planning on inviting the Queen of England!" Margaret said in between the smiles.

"Darling daughter, whatever you want, you can have." Saul said.

"Honey," Margaret called out, "sorry for interrupting, just wanted to ask if he has given you a ring yet?"

"Yes, Margaret, it's a five-carat round diamond set-in platinum, and it's beautiful."

"Just as you deserve," she said, "Well, ok then. Everything is covered. I'm happy for you love."

"Thanks, mum," I said. The word "mum" slipped out my mouth ever so pleasantly. I have not said that word, ever. It felt good to have a mother figure in my life now.

"Alright, sweetness, the night is calling. Marcus, do have a great night and I'll see you both on Sunday." Saul said from the other end of the line as he put an end to the lengthy conversation. We were back to just to us at the dining table and I could not think of any other thing other than how much Marcus loved me the way Joseph should. I refused to think of Joseph anymore and decided to focus more on my blessings. So, I switched thoughts to the platinum ring that graced my fourth finger – which is now a bit heavy. I am sure it cost about half a million dollars, that *is expensive*, I thought, but Marcus would be the last person to care about money, honor, or the way things looked. He loved me and wanted the world to know it.

"Sweetheart, I have one more phone call to make." He said, sipping a cup of milk. He was clearly in this with me; he had utterly refused to be served a bottle of champagne or any other drink during dinner.

"At this late hour?" I inquired. I was sure we should be heading home now. It would be past 10 or 11 p.m. The streets were silent, and the roads seem to have gone to bed. Total silence, like the quiet that surrounded us in this restaurant. The alone time we were having started to make it feel as if we were the last people on the planet. I wanted home, most importantly, to be in his embrace.

"I want to inform my parents. I'll call my grandmother tomorrow." He responded and I just nodded. The phone rang and you could hear a sleepy John Marcus answer, "Son, I hope this is something I need to know at this hour."

"No John, as long as our boy is safe. It must be a pressing issue irrespective of the time." His mum said, trying to calm his dad. I just sat there smiling at such a happy family he had, one I am to join in a few weeks. "Darling, what is the news?" she asked.

"I'm getting married. Samantha has agreed to marry me. And you're going to be grandparents of twins."

"Oh, my God! This is exciting, Marcus," his mum exclaimed over the phone. "This is delightful news indeed!" his dad added.

"We must celebrate this." Isabella furthered, overwhelmed with joy.

"Yeah, I know, mum. Please mama, do me the favor of telling the girls. I will put a call through to Grandma Mathew myself. You can help tell your parents, and I call them later tomorrow too."

"Alright, baby. I'll do just that!"

"Son, I'm a lot sleeper now, do come by tomorrow, let us celebrate, you know, sip some champagne, and I will tell you how to be a good husband and father. Just share all the love, and merriment with your woman tonight. I'll see you both tomorrow." John Marcus added, semi-awake.

"Love you, Dad, and have a lovely night"

"Love you, son," they both responded, and the phone went dead.

I had thought his parents were going to ask a series of questions, trying to fill in the gaps, but with Marcus, everything was that simple. He had once again come to my rescue and cleaned up my mess, but this man never saw it that way. He was everything like Saul was. Marcus said I brought him love and that is all he cared about. My head was whirling. Everything seemed to be happening at the same time: marriage and babies. For the first time in my entire life, I am going to concentrate on being happy and relaxed. Marcus held my hands and suggested we have a little dance after the calls. "I would like to see you move that gorgeous body," he said. I was dead tired; it has been an exceptionally long day. But this was the last man I would say ever want to quiet. He had saved me a lifetime of trouble, the least I could do was dance. One I did with all the joy the universe can hold.

"Sweetheart, I think it's time I get you home, you look really sloppy on the dance floor, it is obvious you are half asleep." My legs were beginning to give away.

"Marcus, I am sorry, I guess with all the excitement I've been through today, my energy is drained," I said, clinging on to his shoulders.

"Well sweetheart, early bedtime and a nap every day comes with carrying a baby. That was my mum's routine when she was pregnant with my sisters. Cutting back on work and a good diet is also essential. And, since these babies are mine, I hope you will not be offended if I want to be involved in everything. I promise not to smother you and you can always tell me to back off." Marcus was so gentle with his suggestions, and there are still things I need to tell him, but not tonight. Tonight, I was just going to enjoy life.

"Your home or mine, my lady?" Marcus said, holding on to me as I continued to cling on to him tightly. We were both wrapped around each other in an embrace. I wanted in on the mood, so I suggested we continue the night at his place. Immediately, he picked up his mobile phone from the table, and after several calls, he held my hands and we were ready to leave. "My home it is," he said with a broad smile on his face.

It was as if the valet at the restaurant could hear all our conversations. We had barely stepped out when the fine young man pulled up Marcus's car. Maximilian saw us out of the restaurant and bade us farewell for the night. He congratulated us once again for the babies. He seemed so excited to have us there and share in our news with him. Marcus led me to his car, showering me with several kisses, getting me more into the cozy mood. I started imagining things in my head. I have it all, I have this man for life. Even dinner tonight was perfect. Marcus always did things on a grand scale when he wanted something; and I was what he wanted in his life, to love me for who I am, to be his companion, his best friend, his partner, his wife, and the mother of his children.

The whole ride home, he would place his hands on my lap. I was tired, but I managed to pat him on his hand so very slightly. It took about twenty-five minutes before we got to Marcus's high-rise building.

It was a fine place to behold. It was clear that Marcus had a taste for something classic. It was written all over the bricks of his buildings. He pulled in front of the building and the attendant was there to open my door. He placed his hand on my shoulder so tenderly and said, "Wait, let me help you out."

He crossed over to my side and lifted me out of the car, holding me in his arms. I was cozy and up for anything he wished to do tonight. He is the man of the year with so many years to come, and I will let him spoil me. He lifted me off my feet and carried me into the foyer and told the attendant to hit the elevator button to the penthouse. I felt like a little girl.

"Marcus, we are not married yet, carrying me over the threshold comes later," I said, wrapping my hands around his neck. He just continued, smiling. He would not drop me and I was enjoying every bit of it. When the penthouse doors opened, he took me past his living room, straight to the bedroom, and placed me on the king-size bed. He began by placing gentle kisses on my neck as he caressed his hands over the whole of my body. I felt his passion as it began to rise.

He continued kissing and gently helped me with my dress, running his fingers over my panties, ever so slightly kissing my lips. His fingers slipped below the silk of my panties. I yearned for him as much as he yearned for me. Marcus retreated and took off his shirt, I sat up to help him with his belt running my hands over his well-built, caramel toned skin. Marcus is built with a body like that of a gladiator, and that excites me.

As soon as he got his pants off, he turned and fixed his gaze on me. I was just in my panties and bra, not far away from being fully naked. Marcus knew what the effects of seeing his naked body had on me. I was lost in ecstasy. He leaned over and kissed me with such intensity that all the tiredness in my body left. All I felt was a burning desire to have him thrust himself in between my legs.

He pushed me back on the bed, making sure I was exactly where he wanted me – laying flat. He had me where I had him the last time, but tonight, the tables had turned, and I am not about to change that. Marcus pulled my panties off and reached around behind my shoulders to unfasten the clip on my bra. I was naked, lying there in front of him. He locked eyes with mine, placed his hand between my legs and opened the folds of my vagina. I took a gaze at his maturity; it was longer than I remember.

Marcus cupped my breast and said to me ever so compassionately, "I want you to know from this day forward, you and these babies you're carrying, are mine. I love you more than life, remember this. I am going to erase every man that was ever here before me." With that statement, I laid there numb, my thoughts of what to come was racking my brain. I just wanted him inside me, and as if he could read me like a book, he kissed me hard and thrust his shaft deep inside with such force I gasped for breath, wrapping my legs around him. It was like he penetrated me to the very core of my womanhood. I could feel him in the whole of my body. The thoughts of my babies spiraled through my head, but it would not last as he continued to thrust himself in me. It was gentle, but so profound. I could feel he was claiming all of me, even my babies.

Marcus continued to pound, rotating, and digging inside me like he was trying to find a lost key. It was amusing to see him thrust so gently, every pound he gave made me was a hunger for more. There was no foreplay; there was no need. The force at which he penetrated was enough to make me explode in pleasure. Moreover, I had been wet all night waiting for him to just have me. Twice, I orgasmed when he began to make some soft sound, moaning ever so softly. I knew, at that moment, he was about to release too. So, I held my legs to his back, I wanted all of him inside me.

In a moment or two, and like fireworks, we both came at the same time. One thrust of his massive shaft and we were holding on to each other like we were holding on for dear life.

Marcus had succeeded in erasing every man that had given me a thrill or took me against my will or used me for my body. Then there was Joseph and his love for me. From now on, my thoughts would only be of Marcus and the joy and satisfaction he brought me. He held me close and whispered, "sleep, my darling, you are growing our babies."

Still cuddled up in the white quilt, I awoke to find Marcus watching me sleep. "Good morning, my love, you look so beautiful. Tell me sweetheart, if you were an artist, how would you paint your future? Put no limitations on what you would paint." He asked. Although I find it strange that the first words I am getting this morning are a question, a series of questions that will lead to other questions, I decided to answer. I rose slightly and propped myself up on my elbow. I painted a picture of me working at my successful law firm, with children crawling around through my office, looking through my books and making it hard for me to work. There will be a husband who would come and help me with my children and take them out from under my feet. There will be a large house where money was not an issue. There will be animals for the children to play with and take care of. Dogs, kittens, rabbits, and a horse. "A happy family." I said, staring at his bare chest laced with thin hairs.

"Samantha, we can have everything you described. Your canvas and mine are the same. But you would not mind if I add that we will also try to teach our kids humanitarian activities and an intense devotion to education. I want them to learn and I have expectations that they challenge themselves. So, you see, you and I seem to be in harmony in most things that are important to us. We are very compatible in bed. We both enjoy having fun in almost all parts of our life." He said, keeping his gaze at me.

"I have been thinking of how perfectly matched we are. I am delighted that you came into my life." He said, stroking my hair slightly. "Last night, I needed to stake my claim. It is selfish of me, but I am adamant about erasing others, especially Joseph, from your life. I guess in some ways, I am glad I played the field, but I am not proud of sleeping with women who had expectations of me. It took me to the age of 32 to find a woman who I wanted to share my life with. I want us, no matter how it may affect our relationship, to speak honestly. If you ever feel I am taking you for granted, please speak up, and I promise to do better." He furthered, planting a kiss in my hand.

Before he could say another word, I interrupted him, "Marcus, I need to tell you about my life before Saul and all of my risky behaviors – something that has plagued every moment of my life." Marcus wrapped his arm around me and said, "I'm listening."

"Marcus…um… you know, when I first met you, I saw you as an arrogant, rich, spoiled man who was given anything he wanted in life. You were so good looking and sure of yourself. You were the type of man I felt like I had to teach a lesson. I thought you would think because I was a woman, independent, well educated, and have my own opinions, that you would think less of me. I wanted to be loved unconditionally, which is absurd because I have since learned that that only happens in parental love, Saul taught me that. So, when I met you, I told myself that I could selfishly have you sexually, and from my history, I used sex more often as a weapon. Sex was a very selfish act that I was good at. I would make men succumb to whatever I wanted. I choose to treat them however I wanted. Marcus, when you took me to your apartment, I had a plan. I knew I was a good attorney and was aware of your father's dealings, but then you showed up and questioned my abilities. So, I drugged you. I do not know if you remember, but I had my way with you. I brought you to the highest of excitement, and then brutally, I pulled back. Do you remember anything about that night?"

"Yes, Samantha, I remember quite clearly you tortured me, but torture is not really the right word. I was wary, but so clearly turned on that I had no care of what you would do next. So, Sam, I have good memories, and it made me want to get to know you."

"You were aware? Even when I cuffed you to the bed?" I asked, putting on a more serious look.

"Well, I was questioning my own sanity at that point, but then you made it pleasurable, I thought, *what the hell?* Honey, I hope you still have those handcuffs."

"Another thing is, I had an abortion. I know it is a terrible thing to do, and I regret that decision; for years, I had nightmares of children's little hands. I made that decision, young and not understanding that there are men who simply want sex, a one nightstand, and no remorse of what might happen from that impulsive behavior. You know, no birth control is a hundred percent effective. So, when I got pregnant, I went to Kenneth thinking that we could share a child conceived out of this impulsive act, but he wanted no part of it and told me to cut it out, it was nothing more than like having a tumor. He tossed me five hundred dollars and dropped out of my life. I was just a new notch on his belt. That furthered my ill feelings toward men, and then there was my biological father who raped me when I was just eleven. All I have ever wanted was to be loved for me."

Marcus shifted his weight on the bed, turning on his side.

"Samantha, where are your biological parents?"

"My father? I have no idea. I know Saul was enraged. I'm sure he did something to him and my stepmother. My mother killed herself. My father was an animal and had abandoned her in a mental institution. She eventually cut her wrist and died in an indigent's hospital. As for Kenneth, he had a construction company in my hometown, so I really do not know what happened to him.

"Now, there is Joseph – the same Joseph you know. We seemed so compatible and were inseparable in law school. When I left law school and came to New York, I really believed him when he said we would be together and that I was the only woman he ever loved. We did not put any restrictions on each other as far as getting our sexual appetites satisfied. I was busy building my firm and spending time with Saul. Time passed so quickly, so much so that I soon thought about Joseph less and less. It wasn't as if he reached out to me often. He was also at the time building his environmental law firm and lobbying for the environment. We communicated occasionally but did not maintain a physical relationship. It had been two years since I had seen him, so when he called and said he wanted to see me, I foolishly, out of the blind love I had for him, obliged. I had the expectation that he was coming to ask me to marry him, as he had promised. Now, I am questioning why I expected so much from him, knowing full well that Joseph lacked an unclouded vision of what he wanted for himself. His parents were pulling at him for politics, but I wanted something different. I wanted something I could call my own and am ready for everything that comes with it. I want a family, with all the stereotypes of motherhood and with some modern notions, too. So, I outgrew him without either of us realizing it. That picture of my future I painted for you earlier exactly what I want. I mean, I am twenty-eight and ready for the next phase of my life, the next adventure. I want to share it with someone who does not just expect me to be there waiting. I need attention and pursuit. I might be exhausting and maybe unrealistic, but Marcus, that's who I am." I said, almost moved to tears.

"Well, my darling, reach under the blanket and feel how much I want you," Marcus replied with his eyebrow raised and with a devilish grin.

I slid my hand under the covers to find that Marcus was fully erect. Before I could say a word, he reached over and kissed me so passionately. I have never been this dumbly in love. His shaft was certainly hungry for me, and the thought of having another round of his pleasure excited me so much I instantly became wet. I felt an insatiable desire for him. Marcus took his time kisses down my stomach until he reached the lips of my vagina; obviously, I was still naked from the night before. He began to lick and pull at my clitoris ever so slightly, turning me on, and I was moaning like a porn star. I could feel the orgasm become thunderous, but before I could burst from pleasure, he moved away and began nibbling on my neck. *This man is keeping me waiting* I thought. I succumbed to his intense probing of my body and it caused me to make loud moans.

Marcus, held my hands above my head with one hand, pinning my legs down so that he had complete physical control of me. He nipped at my breast and then moved his free hand down between my legs and inserted his fingers deep inside me. I was a floating mess. I could not take it any longer, so I took the last of my strength and screamed softly, "Please, Marcus, fuck me," as I retreated to lay down on my back.

Marcus would not have it, he just ignored my desperate request, bringing me to the peak of excitement and then pulling his hands out. This teasing behavior seemed to go on forever. His fingers kept playing with my clitoris, diving in and out. "Please stop. Fuck me." I moaned softly again. He then turned me over on my stomach using his hand to pull me up onto my knees, quickly got behind me, pushed himself deep between my legs and started pounding softly. I wanted it all in and fast, but he was not going to give in. He thrust it in hard, yet gently, but ever so effective from behind that it was reaching the core of my virginal walls. I was at the height of my orgasm when he started pumping hard, making as many moans as I could until we both climaxed. This time I came hard, I felt excited and satisfied at the same time.

Marcus collapsed beside me and I grabbed him with the last strength I had, resting my head on his chest. "Sweetheart, you and I have the same sexual appetites. And I will let you know every day for the rest of our life how much I want you." I smiled, kissing him softly with the whole of my heart.

"We should go take our bath." he spoke. With that, he jumped up and said, "join me in the shower; it is one o'clock. Let us eat and let our friends know that we are engaged and expecting!"

Chapter Five

The Wedding Plans

After we have had a quick shower and dressed for the day, Marcus suggested we go out for brunch. "You should call Rick and give him the news so he can start on the wedding plans. I want to marry you as soon as possible." He pressed, affirming all that he had said the night before.

"Are you sure, Marcus, even if the babies are not yours?" I teased.

Marcus turned to me, this time with a little bit of seriousness in his voice, "Samantha Amanda Weinstein, I am adamant about never hearing again that these babies are not mine. They are mine, now and forever. So, call Rick."

Calling out my name in full just says it all. I picked up the phone and made a call to Rick, he picked it up but sounded more like he was having a nap. Groggily, he answered the phone, "Yes ma'am, how can I help you on this Saturday afternoon?" emphasizing 'Saturday' to let me know it is the weekend. I knew he was just joking, so I pressed on without mincing words. I was hungry so I wanted to hurry off the phone with Rick and go eat. All the thrusting and grinding I had gone through at the hands of Marcus had managed to bring my locomotive engine to a halt.

"Rick, I'm getting married! Marcus asked me last night and I said yes!"

"What! Wait… just like that. I mean, you are pregnant, and you are getting married now? How girl, just how?" Rick said, literally screaming at the phone."

"Yeah… that's the gist of it darling. But that isn't going to happen today." I said, not giving in to his screaming.

"I'm happy for you, girl. I really am. But girl, you better get the details ready for Monday when we see you, I want to know it all, everything." Rick said, still literally screaming over the phone.

"I just wanted to let you in on the news. And just so you know, you will be planning the wedding and you'll be my maid of honor too."

"Hell yes, girl! I'm in charge, just tell me the way you want it and I'll give it to you!"

"Please, inform Scott. I want him at the wedding too. I want a big societal wedding, whatever the cost." I said, sounding a little more like what Rick would want to hear

"Girl, I gotcha," Rick responded over the phone. "You and I will enjoy spending the old farts money. I am assuming we have an unlimited budget for his only child, right? How soon? Have you set the date?" he furthered.

Right there, still on call with Rick, I called out to Marcus. "Darling, the twins are due around June 23rd. So, I am thinking around June 1st?"

"Sounds good, my love," Marcus said.

Rick gushed out his words "I'll get started right away. This will be so much fun. I love you, sister." With that, he hung up and I am sure he will burn the lines up making calls.

As soon as I finished speaking with Rick, Marcus's phone rang and he gave me this curious look, "Yes, sis," he said, nodding his head momentarily.

"Honey, it's Penelope, she wants to congratulate you." I took the phone from him, and his younger sister was giggling over the phone. "Welcome to our humble family, Samantha. We are so glad to have you with us, girl." Almost screaming out of the phone.

"Yes, thanks a lot, honey. Your brother is such a blessing." I replied, with a smile wide across my cheeks.

"My sister and I want to give you a baby and a bridal shower combined. And of course, anything we can do to help with the plans." Penelope continued.

"Yes, that sounds great. I will get in touch if necessary. Thank you so very much." I spoke. Marcus reached for his phone and said, "Little sister, we are on our way out, we'll talk later. Moreover, Dad's planning a party to celebrate the engagement and we will talk about it all, but later, love you," and he hung up.

"I hope my sisters do not overwhelm you."

"No, darling, it's fun to have all this family attention."

"Sam," his new nickname for me, "let us go shopping."

Shopping with Marcus was fun. We went to the nearest mall that had a maternity shop inside. The lady that waited on us was instantly smitten with Marcus. She was under his spell and was very eager to explain the new modern styles of maternity clothes. She brought out pants, blouses suits, and dresses. She showed us formal wear and informal attire. She did not know who Marcus was, but she knew that she was about to make an exceptionally large sale. Marcus sat in a chair looking at baby books and magazines on what to expect at various stages of pregnancy. He wanted all the books. I stopped him short of buying baby clothes, although I found myself tempted.

Sally, our salesperson, offered a card of a designer that she recommended who designs nurseries. Saul had already begun work on the nurseries, but since Marcus's penthouse was bigger, we decided it would be the better place to start our family, until he could find the right house for us. He handed Sally his *American Express* and asked if she would have everything delivered to the penthouse. Sally further recommended birthing classes that she thought we would be interested in. Marcus was eager to get involved in anything that would help with the babies and me. He was going to be an involved father. He handed Sally a $200 tip.

"Are you ready for a late lunch?" He asked.

It was past four and I had almost forgotten all I had today was a cookie and a cup of espresso. I was so hungry. "Yes, let's get something to eat." I was tired but very thrilled.

We ended up in a coffee shop that offered a variety of healthy sandwiches and side salads. Marcus ordered a sandwich with avocado, cheese, and chicken, and a side bowl of fruit. It sounded so good that I ordered the same with a delightful juice to drink. Amid eating and chatting about various other things, Marcus reached for my ring finger and kissed it gently, the diamond glistened. He was having berries when his phone rang, it was Paige.

"Hi sis, what's up?"

"What do you mean 'what's up?'" she said. "I'm getting a sister-in-law and I'm going to be an aunt and I have to hear it from Penelope?" Paige questioned. This time the phone was left on the table on speakerphone.

"I'm sorry, Paige, but I am kind of busy embracing the whole thing myself."

"You better be sorry and get the hang of it. We must celebrate this, man." Paige responded with all the sweetness she could gather.

"Yeah Paige, I understand you want to throw a party. Yes, you should do your thing; I am fully in for whatever. I will send Samantha's number to you. You can call her later in the week with the details. Love you." Marcus responded. As soon as Marcus got off the phone, my cell rang too, it was Rick. We were in for a lot this coming month, and we better get used to it.

"Samantha, Joseph called the office and he wants to talk to you. He mentioned that his grandfather is dying and the old man is asking to see you. I don't know if you would want to talk to him, so I told him I would tell you." Rick blared over the phone

"Thanks, Rick, I will call him." I looked over at Marcus. "I need to go see Joseph's grandfather before he dies." My head dropped down to hide a tear running down my face. I was not sure of what Marcus would say. He had said nothing and just continued chewing at his bowl of fruits. "He loved me, Marcus. Will you go with me?" I suggested. I knew he would not say no.

"Ok, Sam, I will have it no other way, you are to be my wife and the mother of my kids." Those words filled my hearts with anxiety, I just nodded. Joseph was the last person I wanted to see now for all the obvious reasons in the world. If there was anything I was certain of it was that Marcus was going to be possessive, where Joseph was concerned. Joseph would have a lot of questions on why I was marrying so fast after he had broken my heart, knowing that I loved him so very much. Joseph might have found out that I am pregnant, this news travel fast, but I do not wish to tell him that the twins might be his. Joseph had chosen his path, his honorable choice, and I have made mine. I was happy. I leaned forward and kissed Marcus on the lips as I settled for the last thought that crossed my mind – I have a great man in Marcus.

"Can we go home? I think I'm getting fatigued." I said. Marcus did not waste any time. He asked for the bills and tipped the waiter, took his phone and mine from the table and we were on our way.

When we arrived at the Penthouse, Marcus's staff had everything under control. My clothes had arrived and my other things had been brought over from my place. I had decided it was better we move to his place so we could start preparing for the babies. The chef was cooking dinner while I sat in the den, watching TV.

"Sam, why don't you take a shower and rest before dinner? I want to call my grandmother before she hears from someone else." He said, picking up the phone and heading to the balcony. I, on the other hand, was grateful for the time alone. Time to myself to think. I found my way to the bedroom, and instead of launching into the shower, I fell on the bed and asleep.

"Sweetheart, dinner will be ready in minutes, you should take a quick shower now." Was what I heard that brought me back to life. Marcus was just walking into the room. I *must have been asleep for quite some time*, I thought. I sat up and shook my head in agreement with what he said, he pulled me up to my feet and directed me to the shower. He had a glow in his eyes and that boyish grin on his face. When I got out of the shower, laid out was a beautiful black gown, one that was free flowing. He was laying on the bed, beside the gown. He must have bought this while I was trying on clothes. He and the salesperson must have conspired to do this.

"Please wear this gown to dinner." Marcus said. I was a little perplexed, not knowing where this is going because, most often, we ate dinner sitting on bar stools while he cooked. But today, he had his chef prepare the food and was having us served. "Put that dress on, darling, and don't wear any undies."

"No shoes too, I guess?" I said, smiling and reaching for the dress. Underneath the dress was a velvet box. I looked at Marcus and he just nodded. Inside the box were beautiful emerald blue drop earrings. "They are beautiful, Marcus."

"My darling, they bring out the blue in your eyes." He said looking at me seductively. I had already applied lite make-up, and I felt exquisitely dressed. *"Now, that's the way I want you tonight and nights after this, barefoot and pregnant."* Marcus said, whispering those words to me softly. I went to the table that was beautifully set with china and crystal. He pulled out my seat and I appreciated his attentiveness. Our server poured us a glass of wine, just a small amount for me. I checked with the doctor who said a small amount occasionally was not harmful to the babies. The standing rib roast was wonderful, vegetables cooked to perfection, and a wonderful salad. For dessert, we had cherries jubilee; the flame was dazzling. He picked up his glass and professed his love for me saying, "I love you; Samantha and I plan to have many surprises for you and my family." I was treated like a queen and I just sat there enjoying every moment.

Marcus's staff continued to disappear and reappear without instructions. Moments later, after we had finished eating and rested for a little while, we chatted about how our lives are perfectly matched. He led me to the bedroom and closed the door and pulled my black dress over my head. I had no panties on, so I was entirely nude. I felt a little shy standing in front of him. I was beginning to show a little and my stomach was no longer as flat, though I tried to keep fit through exercise every day.

"Sit my love," he whispered in my ear so slightly, his heart racing against mine. *This man has many tricks up his sleeve*, I thought and I was willing to let him reveal all that he had in his arsenal. Marcus began to remove his clothes, very slowly, knowing I was watching and admiring his rugged good looks. He was chiseled to perfection and his dark curly hair and blue eyes were part of the package. His eyes when they glowed of lust, turned a hazel, almost brown color. That was from his hot-blooded Spanish side of the family. His cupid lips were apart, enough to see his perfect white teeth. He already had an erection, which was now his trademark around me. He could never hide his lust for me. He laid his body on top of me, pushing me back against the pillows, I was wet as water. He reached down and pulled my legs up on the bed and was careful to support his weight, to not crush my body. This was not going to be an aggressive sex strike. He was passionate, but gentle. He began by snuggling his face into my neck and then nibbling on my ear. He moved down to my face and kissed each eye before moving my lips apart with his until he engulfed my mouth. I felt him begin to move with a little more urgency as his passion for me increased. He stroked my back and moved his hands around to cup my breast, gently caressing them. I began to moan as the passion was beyond my control. He quickly kissed me on my mouth and said, "I love you, Samantha."

"I love you too, Marcus," I manage to say, gasping for his touch. With that, he gently moved my legs apart and rubbed his shaft up and down the lips of my core. I wanted more, but he clearly wanted this encounter to last more than our usual encounters did. He was making love to me, something I really did not understand until he came into my life. Marcus was not a one-night stand kind of man, nor did he want a relationship based on duty, convince, or lack of commitment. He is in love with me. I can only have this type of love once in my life. He said I was the love of his life and I understood what he meant. We were both past the point of keeping our cool, trying to control the peak of the romance. He held my chin up and kissed it again, and with that, he thrust deep into me. He thrust once, and one more time, until we met each other at the crest of our orgasm. I felt complete, loved. I dug my nails into his back as I held on to him. We fell asleep together, with our bodies intertwined.

The next morning, I reached for Marcus, and he was nowhere around. I stretched like a satisfied alley cat. The night before seemed like a dream.

"Hello, my love, you really slept into the morning," Marcus said, stepping into the bedroom.

"What time is it?" I inquired, still yawning and stretching

"It's past 12 already. I guess you shouldn't keep a pregnant woman up so late, right?" He said, chuckling. I gave him a smile rather than words and stretched again like an alley cat. Mrs. Maggie, Marcus's housekeeper came asking what I would like to eat. She also explained the importance of folic acid on an unborn baby, saying, "seems like you need a lot of it, so I brought you a glass of orange juice." Everyone here is so very polite and carefree, Marcus was as free as a bird.

"Marcus, will you hand me my robe, it would seem I've lost my dress," I said chuckling, wrapping myself with the quilt. The memories of the night before flooded my brain. It was a wonderfully orchestrated sensual night; one I had not ever experienced. It was passionate and lovely. Wrapped up in my robe now, I looked down at my bulging belly, my stomach was no longer flat, placing me at five months. It had been two months since the engagement and things were moving at warped speed. However, my bump was hardly noticeable when I was clothed. I took a long sip of the chilled orange juice. I was very thirsty from the night's activities. Suddenly a wave of nausea came over me. I jumped out of bed and headed to the bathroom. I crouched myself down over the toilet as violent convulsions began to hit me. In less than a minute, my stomach was empty. Marcus hurriedly rushed in with a cold, wet rag and held my hair back as I finished spitting the phlegm from my mouth. I wiped my face, while he helped me to my feet. I washed my mouth out with a glass of water. I was dizzy and leaned against him. The thoughts of having to do this alone flashed through my face like a movie trailer. "Thank you, Marcus." I said without thinking. The doctor had mentioned that I might experience severe nausea occasionally throughout the pregnancy. Marcus held me close and said, "Darling, it is you that has to endure the effects of what I had done to you from a few moments of pure joy. I should be thanking you." He said, kissing my forehead. "I love you, and nothing is more important to me than your health and that of the kids. You are not going through this alone." He furthered. That moment, I thought of Joseph and his choice to see Emily through her pregnancy, no woman deserves to go through this experience alone. The father should be there and support her however he can. Now, I understood why Joseph made his choice; he made the baby, so he wanted to do his part. I understood that now as I leaned on Marcus. He helped me back to bed and over the intercom asked Mrs. Maggie to bring me some dry toast and ginger ale to settle my stomach.

"Darling, I don't want you to see me throwing up in the toilet." I said, shying away, still cuddled up.

"Samantha, keep this thinking up and I'm going to spank you. I am your partner, the father of those babies, and I am where I am supposed to be. You should rest for a while. I am going to make a call to the doctor." He said affirmatively.   Marcus left the room and I snuggled down in the bed. Within a few moments I was fast asleep. I woke up a couple of hours later and felt fine, but hungry. Still in my robe, I headed straight for the kitchen and found Marcus and Maggie having coffee. Marcus was reading construction drawings.

"Hey, sweetness, how do you feel now?" Maggie asked.

"Much better, but hungry." I answered, staring at Marcus who looked up from his drawings. Peg said, "Well, let us take it slow, I'm going to scramble you a couple of eggs and make some dry toast. Let us get some water into you so you don't dehydrate. And maybe a cup of herbal tea?" I sat at the bar next to him, saying nothing. Marcus just leans over and puts his arm around me until my food was ready. The food tasted delicious, as simple as it was. I felt refreshed.

"Sam," Marcus called out gently, "you know today is Sunday, and we are supposed to be at your dads at six. Do you want me to cancel dinner and stay at home?

"No, no, I feel fine. I can get out," I said like I was protesting. Really, I wanted to go out. "Well, the doctor said I should leave it up to you, but you may experience nausea on and off throughout your pregnancy as the fifth month is late to start getting sick. So, if you feel up to going, I am going to take this 1956 bottle of sherry to your dad and see if I can beat him at chess tonight. Let us make it an early night." He said, swinging the bottle of sherry in his hands.

Being with each other for most of the week excited me, but it also made me tense at the same time. We will be leaving for Washington, D.C. on Tuesday to see Joseph's elderly grandfather. I am sure Marcus has things at his office he might want to attend to and I have a few last-minute details at my office that needs my attention.

I used the first working day of the week to tighten up loose ends. The thought of seeing Joseph made me cringe. This would be the first time we would be in the same room since he broke the news to me in Boca. But I had Marcus beside me and I will weather this storm. Later that evening we arrived at Saul's. It was such fun to watch Saul and Marcus interact; they genuinely liked and respected each other, but neither liked losing while I was the spectator – it was quite funny. There were so many laughs and good intellectual conversation between these two men I adored. Margaret made a wonderful dinner for us all; Saul had insisted on steak and potatoes. As much as I sent love messages to Marcus all night, I saw the same for Saul from Margaret. It was written all over him- the love he had for Margaret. Like Marcus, all he ever wanted was a family and a woman that was his equal. Margaret had loved Saul enough to walk away, and that is what Marcus had said he would do if that is what it took to make me a happy woman. I was finally getting a grasp of what it truly means to be loved.

Rick had been taking care of everything at the office and working with the wedding planner in preparation for my wedding, which was scheduled for the first of June. Marcus's darling sisters planned several showers and parties. Saul and Margaret were dealing with a party planner to announce our engagement for some time in April. Everything seemed to be happening all at once; the most interesting, however, is the babies growing in my bellies. Due to my foreseen unavailability at the office, Rick had recommended that we hire an added attorney, we both agreed on one who had worked with the firm in the summer. She had shown great initiative and my clients took a liking to her. But still, a lot of them only wanted to work with me.

Tomorrow, I had two appointments with an old client that was being sued over some boundary disputes, which I hoped to talk him into settling out of court. I always tried to tell my clients that going into court was like rolling the dice; however, the judge felt that day could decide their outcome, no matter how much the law was on their side. This is the reason my retainers were high; sometimes, you may have to grease the wheels to get heard. Other times, you needed to be seen at a social function or a political rally to predict the outcome of the case. I was Saul's daughter and he had taught me well. Like Judge Ford, I had not seen him since the last campaign, the donation my client had contributed had not helped him get reelected. I had heard he was retiring and there will be a new sheriff to take his place. He was young, ambitious, and determined to clean up what he called "corruption." This is another judge that would either be a pain in my ass or Saul's. I could eventually get to know him personally and he would even like and respect my work.

Although I do have some boundaries I would not push, and these had to do with family law. I personally stayed away from it, but I would sometimes aid one of my attorneys who wanted to help a friend. The system for domestic law had failed. What should have been an easy decision, based on information fairness and the law, usually never was. I stayed away from it and stuck with real estate law, where there are no emotions that would keep me up at night.

Marcus also wanted me to meet with his company's bank and a construction firm that was losing a big project. He asked for a meeting at the bank on Monday at noon to see if he could buy out the firm's loans and obtain the property. It was a newly approved subdivision an hour from New York; a hundred acres and all the roads had already been put in. The front entranceway is gated with a guard house and staffed with security to keep only homeowners and guests safely inside the gates. It is zoned for ten-acre tracts. Marcus wanted to build our future home on three tracts, which would make us owners of 30 acres (about half the area of a large shopping mall). He planned on building ten more houses. "One way to spend money, and spend it well, is real estate," he always says. The rest of the land would be common ground. It would have a horse barn, tennis courts, playground, and riding trails. He wanted to build us a family home that was not completely isolated from people. He wanted his children to have friends and us to have neighbors. Of course, he was guaranteeing that his children would be playing with a very selected group of people. He wanted an association board that had to approve the residences that wishes to live there.

Meanwhile, Marcus also wanted his children to engage in humanitarian services and visit places his firm sponsored to understand that they had opportunities that most children did not. He wanted them to go to work with him and learn that with money came more responsibility. He also wanted them safe, so this new project would have sufficient security. He made sure that there was security always close by, just like his father still did for the family; knowing that there were always known and unknown threats to the Matthew's family, then it is reasonable. But still, if Marcus wanted to ride or drive one of his toys, like a motorcycle or sports cars, he did. He did not want his children to be scared, just cautious.

On Monday morning, Rick was the first person to give me a call reminding me of my meeting at the bank. Later that afternoon, I arrived at the bank where Mr. Carr was waiting in the conference room. He seemed extremely uncomfortable, so I decided to put him at ease. I try to understand my clients and I was certain that Matthew's firm, under Marcus's leadership, would give him a fair offer. Marcus had already instructed me to give Mr. Carr the sum of ten million dollars of his debt to the bank, and ask if Mr. Carr could stay on and work as a subcontractor for The Matthew's Group. With a prior understanding of the bank's position, Marcus had worked the numbers with his finance team late last night. My job was to lay it out for Mr. Carr and see if we could get an agreement before Marcus arrived. They had called Marcus in to see if he was interested weeks earlier. They were unwilling to loan Mr. Carr any more money and he does not have the investment capital to move forward; without the investment capital, he stands to lose it all. The bank could simply foreclose once he defaulted.

"Hello, Mr. Carr." I said walking in on the gentle old guy in his early fifties. He had a green cowboy hat on, and his accent, although Mexican, was polished. "I am Samantha Weinstein, the attorney for The Matthew's Group."

"Hi Miss. Nice to meet you." he responded, stretching forth his hand for a shake.

"Nice to meet you too, sir," I said, receiving his hand. We both had our seats opposite each other and I started the conversion. "Before Mr. Matthew arrives, he has asked me to go over the firm's offer to you. I am sure you are going to see that Mr. Matthew has made a very generous offer, given your circumstances, and will assume your debt on the property.

He also gives you ten million dollars over the 30 million you owe; that should clear you from your financial responsibilities."

Curiously looking at the offer, Mr. Carr spoke in an alarming manner. "I don't think this is fair at all! I have invested twenty million more than that. All the challenging work is complete. So, The Matthew's group is going to buy me off a 70-million-dollar investment, from which he put 20 million, and clear a minimum of a 100 million."

"Yes, sir, I think it's a great offer. Moreover, Mr. Mathew's is offering you to stay on as a subcontractor to his firm. That is the gist of the deal. And as you can see, the bank, through their letter, has agreed to these terms." I said, leaving Mr. Carr to figure things out himself.

"Well, I see. I have no choice other than to accept these terms or declare bankruptcy on this project, which is going to wipe me out." He responded, obviously sad.

"Mr. Carr, the offer is great! However, if you have other, better offers, then perhaps, you can give them a thought. But I must be sincere, the Mathew's are quite reasonable people if you ask me, they are offering you not just a leverage on your debt, but also a role as a sub-contractor in the firm."

"Did I ask you? You work for the enemy." The word enemy caught my attention and made me think that there was something a little off with Mr. Carr. I had the research from my staff showing that he had been deployed twice to the Middle East.

"As you can see, there is a certified check from the Matthew's Group ready to go into escrow for you as soon as you have met the terms of the offer and signed." I pressed him, pointing at figures and flipping pages, showing him the terms and conditions attached to the offer.

Mr. Carr took a deep, long breath and nodded, looked at me, and continued looking at the papers. "Can I have my lawyers look these over?" He spoke. Finally.

"Of course, sir. Enclosed is a letter of intent with a two million earnest money check prepared as soon as you are ready to review Mr. Matthew's offer." He looked at the ten-million-dollar certified check and signed the offer. About that time, Marcus came in the doorway, dressed in jeans and a denim shirt; he looked smashing and I wondered if there was any attire at all that he wouldn't look good on him. He was escorted in by the bank president while I stood there smiling. As soon as he walked in, he stuck out his hand to Mr. Carr and said, "Marcus Matthew, Mr. Carr, do we have an agreement?"

"Yes sir, we do. But I am not sure I want to stay on yet as a subcontractor. I would like to discuss that with my wife." Mr. Carr responded, taking Marcus's hands.

"Certainly, I wanted that offer to be there for you. In case you do not have any more projects right away. I can always use the help, and I know your people might like the opportunity to keep working." Marcus replied nicely.

"Like I said, let me talk to my wife and get back to you."

"Alright, sir." Marcus said as he signed all the necessaries, including the bank's agreement, and except for a few formalities, the deal was official. Marcus shook hands all around, even with me, and it felt a little strange.

"Just let my attorney know if you want to sub-contract some of the projects." With that said, he walked out of the bank. I could not help but think of how professional he was, he would not even acknowledge me as his. So, this was how it was to work for your husband. Professionalism all the way.

Chapter Six

No good in goodbyes

After Marcus had left, I finished business with the bank's lawyer. I made my way out to my car to drive to the penthouse. On my way, I got a call from Marcus congratulating me on the deal.

"Congratulations, my sweetheart. Now, you know where we will be living. I just have to build us a house."

"Marcus isn't that too much for a home? All I want is a master suite with his and her bathrooms and dressing rooms with two large walk-in closets."

"Sweetheart, I want 17 bedrooms and bathrooms. You can call it a castle or anything. You know I love space, and we will need a lot of that with the kids." There was to be no reasoning with him. He is from a wealthy home, not that I was not. But, with the kind of figures attributed to the Mathew's, you cannot expect any less. "Ok, honey… I trust you to build us the right home."

"Alright, sweetness. I will have our architecture draw up plans and then you can make whatever modifications you want. Consider this one of my wedding presents for you."

"One," I said, perplexed.

"Yes, I have to match my gifts with what you're giving me - your heart and two kids. That's unimaginable gift to me."

"Marcus, don't know what to say, really"

"You don't have to say anything, honey," he replied with a loud chuckle.

"Alright, sweetheart. See you at home. I love you so very much," I said, hanging up the phone. The thought of leaving tomorrow for Washington to see Joseph's grandfather consumed my mind during the remaining drive home. Marcus had arrived a little late, and although he had me cuddled up all night, I had an apprehensive feeling that something might go wrong. However, I was glad Marcus would be with me and help me get through whatever Joseph tried to pull. Hopefully, nothing will happen.

I wished tomorrow never came, but it did anyway. We landed at the Reagan airport around 11.00 a.m. and there was a car waiting for us with a driver to take us straight to the hospital. The pilot, Mike, and the head of Marcus's security team had made the trip with us. Mike had been with Marcus since his college days and they were close. Mike had been married before but did not have any children. He was a loner and was happy staying close to Marcus; he was one of the very few people that was, dear to Marcus. Arriving at the hospital, I asked to be led to the intensive care unit where Joseph's grandfather was trying to recover from yet another heart attack. This was his third and his condition had been on and off for a while. The nursing crew had mentioned that he was feeling a lot better today and that he was looking forward to seeing me. The old man was without his family members. I was told they had left for a while to let him rest before I visited him. Joseph's family knew how much Mr. Claiborne had wanted me and Joseph to marry. He was so fond of me; liked my spirit. He would usually joke with his grandson, that if he did not propose, then he might have to do it himself.

I entered the room, so glad to see him setting up in bed, even with an oxygen mask you could see his broad smile.

"Hello, Mr. Claiborne, it's been a while," I said, walking over to him and giving him a hug. I took my seat beside his bed, close to him.

"Oh! Samantha darling, you know I want you to call me Joe. How about a kiss for this old Joe!" He said, winking at me; he was such a bunny.

Joe had always been a lady's man since ancient times. He and Saul are good friends as they had been in the same circles for a while. Joe had his heart stolen at a much younger age, got married, and settled down. Saul, he just continued chasing his political aspirations. Old Joe was the opposite of who Saul was; he was more into raising his family than making money. When Joseph came along, Joe was delighted to help raise his grandson, since his son, Joseph's father, traveled all the time. He said he wanted to raise one child that would follow his own dreams and not someone else's.

"Joe, how do you feel? You look like you can do cartwheels now." I said, finally granting his request and pecking him on his cheeks.

"Great, great, I feel great now that you're here."

"I'm glad to hear that, Joe. I'm glad you are getting well."

"Yeah, I am."

"I'm glad, Joe. It's nice to see you after all these years." I spoke.

"I know, Samantha. I know and that is why I called for you. I must do right by you. You know, I want to talk to you about my grandchild, Joseph." He said, pausing for a minute. I just rubbed his hand gently, making sure he was okay. I just knew it was about Joseph, this old man loves me to the bone, but it is what it is.

"Samantha, I know he broke your heart, and I… wish he had handled things a lot differently. He loves you, no doubts. But, you see, Joseph has been pulled by his parent's aspirations and my take on following his dreams. So, he fell into a hole, and when all that happened, he tried to do the most honorable thing, which is just the easy thing to do. They could have called it a mess that could have just as easily ended with him helping raise the child. He could have still asked for your hand in marriage. I just thought that was the reasonable thing to do, you know? But he has his parents and hers and he just could not handle the pressure. I just wish he had come to me. You know those female tears will get you every time." He furthered.

I just sat there, head bent, and said nothing. I know how Joe feels about me and all that, but that would not matter now. We all make choices. Some we must live with it till the grave. Seeing that I was quiet, Joe continued, "Samantha, you know I know you. You love my boy, and you made it easy for him to throw crap at you, you come across so damn tough and at the same time, vulnerable."

My face lit up; Joe was right. Joseph had all my buttons and he pressed it at will. Regardless, I just sat there with Joe, patting his hands gently "I see that you have no words to say, Samantha." Joe continued picking his word ever so carefully. "I understand… I know you are a fighter, a survivor, and I have never doubted your abilities; that is why I wanted you so bad for my boy. All the same, I am glad you came, I just wanted to tell you myself how I felt. I can understand how you feel." Joe said, this time staring into my eyes for a response, for anything.

"Joe, I am all right. At least, I'm getting there." I spoke. After pausing for a little while, I continued. "Actually, I met a man who I'm getting married to pretty soon. It was tough to take in, Joe. I loved Joseph and you know that is why it was easy for him to always leave me hanging and jump back on the train and make it seem that everything is all good. But the heavens aren't done with me – not yet." I said, smiling slightly, trying to hold back the tears. "Joe, I am expecting a baby – actually, twins. I wanted you to know, but I do not know if Joseph knows. My fiancé and I will be married by June, and I am happy. My heart is finally relieved of Joseph."

"Oh, that's great, Samantha. I'm glad you're happy and moving on, that's really good." He said, his voice waning off gently. We had few conversations, catching up on old times. He never bothered to ask any question with regards to the babies, not that I was willing to give details, but it saved me a great deal. Joe just congratulated me, emphasizing on how much a good mother I will be. I kissed him on the cheek again, leaving him to get some much needed rest, seeing that he was getting weary. As I was walked past the door to where I had met with Joe, I saw Joseph coming down the hallway and I wish the ground would open and swallow me up for a while. *There's no escaping this* I thought. Marcus could have been my savior this time again, but that does not seem a reality now; I left him at the visitor's lounge where he would be waiting for me.

"Samantha," Joseph said, walking up to me with some pace. "I wanted to see you. You would not take my calls, and except for the one time we talked briefly, I have not heard from you." He said, staring straight into my eyes.

"Joseph, it's been a while." I said, trying to ignore his complaint. Now, he stood in front of me, making sure I stopped moving ahead. "Why won't you answer my calls?" he asked.

"There's nothing to talk about, Joseph. Really."

"Samantha, I'm sorry. I know…" before he could say another word or ask any more questions, I responded.

"Apologies accepted," I said with a smile on my face. "Moreover, I'd like you to meet someone." I furthered, walking past him and heading towards the visitor's lounge. Joseph just walked behind me in amazement, at the way I handled the whole situation. I was proud of myself. We walked briskly together to the visitors' lounge. Marcus stood up as soon as he saw me approaching.

"Joseph, meet my fiancé,' Marcus Matthew. Marcus, Joseph Claiborne." I said, kissing Marcus. The two men shook hands as Marcus occupied himself beside me. Marcus said, "Sorry about your grandfather, Joseph. I hope he gets a lot better."

"Thank you. I am glad you could make the trip with Samantha, even though it was prompt. My grandfather really adores Samantha. He would not stop asking for her ever since his health deteriorated."

"Well, it helps to have a company jet at her disposal," Marcus replied, handsomely with a large smile.

"Oh, and congratulations on your marriage and your child. I know Sam and I are looking forward to married life." Marcus said, getting tired of just standing. Marcus was stylishly squaring off with Joseph, and Joseph was hiding his surprise about our engagement well.

"Thank you, Marcus. I really do appreciate you guys coming over." Joseph responded kindly, trying to hide his surprise still.

"You're welcome, Joseph."

"Marcus, do you mind if Samantha and I get some coffee in the cafeteria. I would like a little time with her before she leaves."

"Come off it, man. Samantha is a grown woman; I think you should just ask her. If she is good, I'm good." Joseph made the eye gesture as if throwing the question at me without saying a word. I understood, so I turned to Marcus and said, "Sweetheart, could you give us thirty minutes, and then I will be ready to go."

"Sure, Sam. How about I check on the plane and I will be back in a few." Marcus walked away and Joseph and I caught the elevator to the cafeteria. There was a lot of coldness between us; I would not say a word.

We got to the café and got us a seat at the center. "So, it's Sam," Joseph said, breaking the silence.

"Yes, its Sam. You know Marcus is very laid back, and Sam is a name he calls me for his use only."

"Ok, great. What would you like to have?

"Coffee. No, herbal tea, please."

"Alright then, I will be right back," Joseph responded as he left for the attendant. The cafeteria was mostly vacant. A few people were eating and talking quietly. People came here to talk about the condition of their loved ones in the hospital. I was here to listen to the man who broke my heart and one I had loved since law school. I am a lot better now, I have a caring and loving man who would stand with me even when I am in shambles. But I wanted to give Joseph a chance to explain, knowing that it would not matter. I knew that Emily should not go through the pregnancy alone – no woman should. So, it is all right for Joseph to do the respectable thing and support her, it is the right thing to do.

My question, to him, however, was easy. Did he take responsibility just to be responsible or to make himself look better? That was the only question I needed him to answer, not that it will make any difference now, but at least, I will know. I thought I knew Joseph; I believed him all my life. There was no doubt the love he had for me, but for whatever reason. He had made the decision he made and it showed he never loved me enough. He came back with my cup of tea and his coffee. "Thanks," I said, while he took a seat across from mine. He had hardly sat down when he began speaking. "Samantha, I know I've hurt you really bad and I know now that I could have gone about it differently without having to marry Emily. I know… I know I broke your heart, Samantha!" Seeing that I just continued sipping from my cup and saying nothing, he continued. He reached for my hand, which I let him hold. You never hate someone you have loved that much, do you? I still have a small amount of love for him, but the current that normally went through me and started that fire between my legs, was not happening.

"Samantha," he continued. This time I gave him a little attention. I wanted to hear all of what he had to say. "I always thought it was the right thing for you to go back to New York and start your law firm and be close to Saul. I thought I needed to follow my own career path in environmental law and get my head on straight about what I wanted, personally. I really meant for us to be together someday. I got busy, and it was easy to keep going through the motions of trying to figure out what I wanted."

"I understand that is not an excuse to keep you waiting on hold. I took you for granted, thinking you would always be there for me. Like you have always been. I was a fool to ask you to keep waiting while I sorted out my mess. You deserved more than that. I was selfish not to tell you right away and make you wait, wonder, and believe that my trip there was to ask you to marry me. I got scared… Samantha. I did not want to lose you and the incredible person you are. I loved you for so long that it never dawned on me to think about your expectations or even ask you about what you wanted. I am sorry." He said, his eyes becoming teary. However, he would not stop talking.

"I cannot believe we are done, like really done, Samantha. I know I hurt you to your soul, but I do not think it is that easy for you to move on, just like that. I know there is more to this story of yours and your so-called fiancé, falling in love. And you are getting married already? Tell me this isn't true, Samantha." He furthered, this time, holding on to the tears.

"Joseph, you know your actions and the whole drama caused me to understand that we are two hearts in two different places. I realized that on the trip. It was blinding to me. I wanted marriage, children, a family who accepted me for who I am. I am not the right person to fit into a cleverly arranged expectation from others – your parents for sure. I sometimes need attention, my life is messy and has been messy, so I need someone who loves me just for who I am. Not for who I could pretend to be. I am a good person and I do not want to have to prove myself to anyone. Can you really see me as being second to whatever life you choose for yourself? Be it political or saving the dolphins? I want to be first in my husband's life and I want him to be first in mine. I want kids. And I know now I need to be with a man who knows what he wants and goes after it" I said, trying to keep a straight face, but my eyes would not have it.

Joseph held on to my left hand, wiping his eyes with his right. "Joseph, you'll always be a piece of me, but you and I are in two different places. Your life with Emily will help you clear up in your mind about what you genuinely want. Emily should not go through this pregnancy without the support of the father of her baby. I want you to think also of what you asked of her, to be married to a man who loves and wants another woman. I will not do that to her. Love her Joseph for the mere fact that she has your baby." I said softly. I did not know what to expect, I just wished he had let me be, but the Joseph I used to know, did not. Instead, he pulled my left hand to his lips and held it there. "Samantha, it hurts too much to lose you… and now, you're getting married?"

"Well, I am. Marcus is the man for me; he's exactly what I need at this stage of my life. I am twenty-eight years old and ready for the next chapter. That man, Marcus, he loves me. And we are exactly at the same place. He wants a home, with a good woman as his wife, and kids, and it just happens that I want the same." I responded, smiling at Joseph, looking directly into his eyes.

"It is that simple, you know. He said he knew that from the first dinner we had were together. He wanted me to be his wife; I did not have to go out there in the wild looking for him. He was a son of one of my new clients, and when he found me in my office self-destructing, all he wanted to do was take care of me. And I really want to be pampered, Joseph. I want a relaxed, happy life." I continued, watching how he bent his head and raised it, back and forth momentarily, but still would not let go of my hands.

"You know, there was no way we could work, if you choose to be a politician. I do not see myself becoming a politician's wife. I must be first, and I cannot dress up and put on a happy face because that is what you need for your political plans. Joseph, I love you, but I have grown in spirit since Boca. I know what I want and who I want this life with. And yes, I love him. I do not have to compete with anything in his life. I know where I stand at all times." I said, taking my hand off his.

"I wish I can say I'm sorry, but I'm not. Please, try to make your marriage work, Joseph. Give your marriage a chance; she will be the right match. There were so many things we did not discuss what we wanted in life. This was my fault as well as yours. I was waiting, you were waiting, and neither of us was willing to communicate our life plans. Now it has been settled by actions that were not meant to harm anyone - especially your unborn child. Mine will work, that I am sure of." I said, sitting my ass back against the chair, feeling relieved.

"Samantha, I know there's more to your engagement than you're saying." Joseph replied, his word struck me like lightning. "Don't you think I, of all people, know you too well? You look like you've added a few pounds, I hope it isn't what I'm thinking." Immediately, as those words flew out his mouth, I knew there was trouble. Fortunately for me, Marcus was coming toward us, so I said, "I do not know what you are talking about, Joseph. He loves me, and I love him, and we are getting married. The least you can do is be happy for me and not rambling on about how I gained a few pounds. That is because I have peace of mind now, compared to when I wasn't sure of my future with you." At that moment, Marcus arrived our table, "Sweetheart, are you ready." He inquired.

"Yes, honey. I was about to stand up when you came along." I spoke planting him with a kiss, infuriating Joseph even more.

"The weather is turning bad and I don't want to risk flying, so I booked us a suite and thought maybe you like to catch a show at the Kennedy Center?"

"Alright, honey, that's a great idea," I said. I turned to Joseph, he was still seated and looking at me in bewilderment. "I should be on my way now. Extend my regards to Joe when he wakes." Joseph stood up himself, stretched his hand at Marcus, "Thanks again, for making it here," he said. His eyes flaming red. Marcus, seeing that Joseph's eyes were red, replied to him kindly, trying to calm the situation. "It's a pleasure, Joseph, my man. Once again, I am sorry about your grandfather, and if there is anything we can do, please kindly give us a call." he replied, shaking his hand. I gave Joseph one last hug. "Goodbye." I whispered, as he stood there. Joseph wanted to say more to me, but Marcus had stood his ground and had enough with Joseph. He had his chance, Marcus thought, the man just blew it.

Marcus would not wait any longer, so he grabbed me by the side and held my coat out for me. As I put it on, Joseph pulled me to himself once again, hugged me, and kissed my hair. "I'm sorry we have to go. I'll stay in touch with your grandfather." I said again, affirming that it was over between us.

"Samantha, I will find out whatever it is you're hiding… I promise you." Marcus turned red, looked at Joseph, and said, "look man, we have to go. Samantha is tired. I'm losing patience and you may want to see your grandfather before visiting hours are over."   Joseph stood there while we turned and walked out the front door of the hospital, where Mike and the driver were waiting. I knew Joseph was watching me, and expecting me to look back at him, but he does not matter anymore. The one that matters is beside me.

Marcus led us to the car, he had tickets to the Kennedy Center, where Adele was performing. We settled in the rear seat of the car while Mike took a seat beside the driver. "How did you arrange tickets for Adele's concert? I'm sure it must be a sold-out concert." I asked.

"Well, it pays to be me, doesn't it? Adele and I go back. Met her when I was roaming in Europe. I ran with a group of notable musicians and children of elite families. Some of us were pretty messed up, and others, like Adele, had a good influence on us. I would not say I was one of the messed-up kids, with drugs and all. But I did my share of attending parties and getting dirty." Marcus replied with a cheap smile on his face.

"She agreed to sing at our wedding, and Elton called and said he would love to stand up for me, along with Mike." I was astonished for a minute, but I had realized, that with Marcus, comes a lot of surprises, and I should just get comfortable with it. So, I just smiled and said, "That's awesome. I love you, Marcus."

We got to the concert and were treated to the VIP section, and what a night! Amidst the screaming and shouting, Adele serenaded us with her beautiful voice. She took us through some of the best songs she ever recorded from, "Hello," "Rolling in the Deep," "Someone like you" and "I Set Fire to the Rain", and many more. It got me thinking about Joseph and all the pain he must feel. He was married to someone he might not love as much, and I might as well be carrying his baby for another man. I could no longer hide the anxiety on my face and Marcus could see it.

"Sweetheart, do you need some alone time?" He understood that I needed time to collect my thoughts about Joseph and what kind of relationship we could have, if any at all.

"You do not mind?" I replied, sounding sad.

"No, sweetheart. It is fine. Mike can take you back to our hotel suite and then me and Mason (Marcus's driver. Marcus had sent Mason a head to check out the security of the hotel and pick-up a car for the three of them, before they arrived in Washington D.C.. He was a part of the security team and a valued member that Mike and Marcus had trust in). can grab a late-night sandwich." He replied gently. He kissed me on the side of my head, a gentle kiss. His loves me, so deeply and securely. I loved him, too.

By the time we got to the hotel, there were only a few thoughts on my mind, most of which were centered around Joseph and the kids. *I hope Joseph never makes a fuss of this.* I thought to myself. However, I had accepted the fact that he left me, and not the other way around, which is usually the way it happened. I had explained everything to Marcus, yet, I had this strong feeling that things might go haywire. I knew that everything worked out the way it was supposed to. Joseph was not the right man for me. Saul knew, but allowed me to find out on my own, as painful as it was.

Mike led me to the room we where we were staying for the night, "Have a sweet night, Samantha. If there is anything you need, do not hesitate," he said, closing the door behind him. It was the first time ever Mike had called me by my first name. He was smiling yet he was ever so serious.

As soon as he was gone, I got sleepy. I was asleep when Marcus finally got in. As quiet as he tried to be, he woke me by opening the door and gently closing it. He went into the bathroom to remove his clothes and get ready for bed. He slid in beside me, and I turned to him and said, "thank you." He just reached for me and held me close. I soon drifted back to sleep. I felt taken care of. That revelation to myself was one of the first truthful thoughts on my path to knowing myself. I had fought all my life to be independent and told myself that I did not need to depend on a man. That was one reason I went to law school. I was so competitive and so tense. I created an anxiety-filled lifestyle because I fought what I really wanted most. I wanted to be a woman who needed attention. I wanted to be pampered. I wanted to depend on a husband that was always there to help clean up my mess. I wanted it all. Work, family, and a spouse who understood me and let me be me. Marcus was that man.

The next day, we had a casual morning. He woke up and started caressing my breasts and kissing me. I knew he was hard, but just as gentlemanly as ever, he waited for me to give him the go that everything was all right with us.   I responded by reaching under the covers and massaging his erect cock. He spontaneously engulfed my mouth with kisses and moved on top of me, supporting himself carefully, parting my legs with his. I was already wet, waiting for his cock to slide into me; I never needed much foreplay with Marcus. Our sexual attraction for each other was that intense. I wanted him so badly, but Marcus was going to have a long one and make me wait. He kissed me from my head to my toes, licking every part so intensely and so sexually. I could see from where I lay his fully muscled chest and erect shaft, and it turns me on even more. The same way he kissed, using his tongue to tickle me from my head to my toes, he did the same again, but this time from my toes to my lips, driving me wild. I was already moaning for him slightly as he kissed and caressed my left breast. He slid himself between my aching legs and slowly began to move back and forth. I was feeling every bit of him and I did not know when I said, "baby, fuck me harder." Marcus instead moved rapidly, going fast and slow, rolling and turning, causing my head to spin, and then he began to move more quickly. My clitoris began to twitch; I was raising myself to the peak of my satisfaction. And then he did the most unpredictable thing, bites my ear gently, and whispered, "will you marry me?"

I gasped, "yes, yes… please fuck me harder." And then, all hell broke loose. He began thrusting and pounding me so hard. I started screaming, as quietly as I could. I was trying to hold back the roar. He brought me to orgasm and I could feel him tense up, signaling that he, too, was about to reach his pleasure. He fell face down beside me while I cuddled close to him. We rested until I started feeling hungry. The hotel had a nice breakfast. I had a cup of tea, Marcus had coffee with some slices of bread and egg-white omelet. Mike must have had something similar, but I never bothered to ask; he is a man of few words.

We left the hotel in the late morning, and within moments we were in the jet, heading home. Then it struck me, *I can have it all with this man. I just must accept it and embrace this new journey.*

We were flying mid-air and Marcus was trying to sleep after we had a chat about how last night went without me. Marcus gave me the full gist and I told him of how Mike was nice to me when he dropped me off at the hotel. We all had a laugh and a sumptuous meal as the pilots did their jobs. Marcus was on a business call when I started drifting, my eyes were tired from the morning sex, I presume. But before I could rest, the babies began to move. I was excited and reached for Marcus's hand, and he just smiled. The doctor had revealed to us on my last visit, that the second baby was also a boy. We were going to have twin boys. Dr. McCullough was so understanding with me as a patient and as a woman. She also knew that Marcus could not be the father and as most men, they want a son. Marcus was happy but would not have cared if the babies had been girls. He loved them because they were a part of me. I was so blessed to have a man who loved me for me.

Chapter seven

The Wedding Party

Seven months in and there was no way to hide that I was pregnant. My tummy was huge! I had stopped visiting the office, Rick was in charge, and he constantly called in to give me updates on the wedding plans. This time he called to set an appointment for another fitting for my gown. My body seemed to be exploding now much quicker. I became overly conscious of how I look and if Marcus would find me less attractive. Instead, he kept assuring me that I was more beautiful with the huge boys occupying space in my body – I loved it.

He also always awoke with a hard-on and always reached for me. Sometimes we had to be as creative as possible; he did not want to hurt the babies or me. Often, he simply lifted my body up around him, in a seated position. Sometimes he entered me from behind. Things were going well. I just had to accept the fact that somebody, other than Saul, loved me for me.

Rick would call about the list of attendants that we had decided on. I had four bride's maids, a maid of honor, two junior bridesmaids, two flower girls, and a ring bearer. I wanted a big fancy wedding that spoke to who I was. Marcus had so many friends and family that it was extremely easy to come up with the numbers. He already knew that Elton was coming from Europe. His oldest son was going to be a ring bearer. Then there was Mike and several college friends that I was yet to know. I had asked Tony, my one friend from my past life that was always there for me, to be my maid of honor, in addition to Rick. I had so few friends. I wanted to include everyone that had ever shown me kindness to be a part of my celebration. Marcus's two sisters were also going to be bridesmaids. I had two lawyers from my office that I was especially fond of and they had agreed to join in. Rick was becoming frustrated, even though he made every change, he never complained. He just kept adding to my list and he knew that Saul did not care what he spent to make me happy. It was my day, no matter how crazy my request became.

Marcus had two cousins that were his Aunt Mary's children that were going to be bridesmaids. His dad had three sisters and they had all asked to take part. His Aunt Stephanie had two girls to be bridesmaids. Marcus asked me if two teenage girls from the shelter he supported could be junior bridesmaids. I knew how he wanted these girls to be a part of something like this, to feel important for once. That was fine with me, just as he accepted me for who I was, I accepted him for who he is. I was lucky to find a man who flaunted society and did what he thought best. Having money allowed this man to make choices that not everyone understood or approved of. Saul's lovable wife, Margaret, had two young granddaughters who I had asked to be my flower girls. Saul and Margaret secretly eloped a few weeks back. Saul would always do things his way. A big splashy wedding was not something he and Margaret desired. I just wished I had been there to witness their love as they exchanged vows. So, the list was perfect.

In between the preparation for my big day, Saul had his engagement party. The party was a huge gathering. More than a hundred people came to wish us well. Even though we had asked that donations be made to the charitable organizations we sponsored, gifts came anyway. However, that is not to discredit the gifts. Imagine what to give a couple who had everything? There were gifts included a pure breed horse, works of art, a loan of a two-week stay at a family villa, and many other creative gifts. Margaret, along with Saul's secretary, dutifully logged in every name and the gift so that they will be able to send out a 'thank you' note. Marcus's dad had invited us all to a family dinner party with just the Matthew's and, of course, Saul and Margaret. I still do not know all their names and how they are related. Sisters, brothers-in-laws, uncles, and cousins. It was about 45 people in total and they all had that same Matthew's charm. They welcomed us into the family and no one guessed or asked any question surrounding the paternity of the babies.

We had agreed to get married at St. Francis Cathedral. It would be able to hold the 150 guests that had were invited to the wedding ceremony. There were five hundred invitations sent out between the wedding guests and the reception guests. We had decided to hold the reception at the New York Public Library, as all expenses for the venue went to support the library. We would be in the Barro's Forum, a very elegant part of the building. The views of the city would be breath taking. Limos and hotel accommodations needed to be made for all the out-of-town guests, as well as transportation to the cathedral and the reception venue. Rick had hired Geller Events to make sure every detail was elegant, sophisticated, and as cohesive as possible. In all of this, I let Rick continue to plan my wedding as if it were his. Rarely did I disagree with his choices; he knew me and my tastes. With all that Rick was doing, managing the office and having to plan a big wedding, that made me adore him even more. As the weeks went on my delivery date got nearer. I began to slip away to my old apartment. Sometimes I napped, and other times, I just looked out the window, questioning my decisions, asking myself if I was moving too fast.

Since Joseph and I had parted from the hospital cafeteria, he had not tried to reach me. And I had been so thankful for his silence. Marcus himself had been busy with building our dream home. He was happy in his element, and I simply let him make all the decisions concerning the house. I knew it had seventeen bedrooms and a few more bathrooms. It came with a six-car garage and all kinds of areas for maids, nannies, cooks, and staff that would be needed to run a house of that size. Sometimes I was so overwhelmed that I would only tell Rick I was not coming in. Not that I did it often, but on days I would plan to leave for the office, I would just go numb and find my way to the park or have lunch by myself. The babies were a constant reminder of how my life was changing and the mess that would have to be figured out once they were born. Of course Marcus claimed that they were his no matter the color, but only Saul and I had talked about the real possibility that they were Joseph's. That fact plagued me. Was I being fair to them and Marcus? I had wanted to wait until after they were born to get married; but Marcus would not have it. He said it did not matter who the biological father was, they would have his name and no one would question their paternity, at least not within our circle. He had a public relations firm that handles all good and bad publicity concerning the Matthew's Group and he had promised that if there were a need for it, they would sweep into action. Marcus was out of town bidding on a thousand acre horse farm in Wyoming, that at one time belonged to a billionaire in Las Vegas, and he wanted it as another wedding gift to me. Money made a significant difference in the way folks like the Matthew's made decisions. All the while the thought of having a doctor perform a DNA blood test on the unborn twins for paternity haunted me to the depth of my soul. I was not sure if this would not escalate to a bigger problem in the future, especially if Joseph found out. However, I had gotten advice from doctors that DNA testing babies in the womb came at a risk and could cause me to go into early labor sooner than expected, so I refused the test. Sometimes, I questioned if I was just afraid to find out the truth.

Two weeks before the wedding, I decided that I was going to stop all activities related to stress. Marcus and I had decided to work from home. Everything was ready, and although I felt as big as a house, the doctor said my weight was perfect, I would be on track to deliver around the 23rd of the month. All the nurseries were ready for the twins and we had hired a nanny that I really liked. There were overly tensed days, but Marcus stood by me through it all.

Days rolled by and soon the big day was here. I could not help but feel for Rick. He was a perfectionist and was doing all the running-around. Two days to the wedding, Rick came down to Marcus's, where I have been for the past several months, to tell me that everything was ready. It was the night of our rehearsal dinner and we were down to the wire. In two days, I would be Mrs. Mathew - June came too soon.

Our home too, was coming along. Marcus had closed contracts for five more families to build in his new subdivision. He closed the Wyoming deal, and we are now the owners of a thousand-acre horse farm. I wanted to see it for myself, but Marcus refused for me to fly – everything seemed to be happening at the same time.

Marcus's dad had insisted the rehearsal dinner be held at the Mathew's mansion. We all thought it was a reasonable idea since it will not be that far from the cathedral. The night was perfect, the weather was cozy, yet chilled, and even though I was heavy, I found it all fun. We arrived at the Mathew's home later that afternoon and everything for the night was ready. I had a red dress with gold-colored flats to carry me through the night. The red dress was so flowy, you would not even know I was wearing slippers! It was the logical thing to wear. I was eight and a half months pregnant. Marcus, on the other hand, was dressed in a double-breasted black lapel suit, with a black belt and Buchanan leather shoes. I could not imagine my man any more handsome.

We had everyone in the family there, except for Rick, who was around, but was not at the table. However, his partner, Scott was sitting with the other family members. Everything looked glamourous, and for the first time, I saw how Saul could be. He was dressed in a navy and grey suit, and he looked captivating. What caught my attention was his hairstyle – he had a more modern look compared to how he a styled his hair, which was usually combed all the way back. Margaret must have talked him into trying something to look a little bit younger, and it worked. Due to my heaviness, I had become a woman of less words; I got irritated easily, but I knew it was all part of the package. Over the months, I had mastered how to keep a smile, even on my worse days.

Marcus and I joined everyone at the table. We were the last to sit and walked in with Penelope, who was as dazzling as her brother. I was not particularly interested in a large party, ours look like a banquet for Roman emperors. The dinner was held in the gardens, under the cherry trees that graced the Mathew's garden. It was decorated with yellow, glowing light making for a colorful and unique atmosphere. Isabella and John were looking dashing – Marcus's old man sure knew how to turn up, even though he was dressed in less than formal attire. We were all merry and shared moments of laughter and joy. Marcus and I were asked questions surrounding our relationship and it was all fun. There was a toast to us, which delivered by Isabella. I know where Marcus got all the finesse from – she was stunning, shinning, a perfect queen for John. I hope I could live up to that. Finally, I felt like I had the big family I had craved all my life. I was home.

The dinner continued into the night. Most of the time I was just there; smiling and eating everything there was to eat. A little of everything will not hurt, I suppose. I will need a lot of strength the next day anyway.

The wedding plans were finished, Rick had made sure of that. He had selected Justin Alexander, a local designer renowned for making unique gowns that fit the personality of the bride, to design my wedding dress.

I had chosen a ballroom style gown. It was a lace and chiffon gown with a sweetheart neckline. The lace had appliques placed on the skirt flowing down to a beautiful chapel train. Its underlining, free-flowing skirt was cloudy blue. Saul had given me pearl earrings and a pearl necklace to go with the diamond ring on my left hand, and a pearl and diamond bracelet on my right hand. I had chosen to wear my hair up with a simple, contemporary design adorned with the same material as my dress. My shoes were cloudy blue satin. I felt so beautiful in this dress, and it was perfect for my bulging stomach. I did not care that I looked eight months pregnant. However, I was tired much of the time. Rick had made sure that I had a lounging couch in my dressing room and water so I could take a break during the festivities.

The morning of the wedding was crazy. I was fidgety and tired, filled with anxiety. And at the same time, excited that I am getting married to a man who adores me. The cathedral ceremony was supposed to last just a few hours, so Marcus had planned that we leave after an hour so I could go home and rest. I had Penelope and Rick by my side all through the service; they were such an immense help. Paige had also done her share. After they had given me an assurance that everything was good and going well, I settled down. Soon I was dressed in my overflowing sky-blue gown. I took a peep in the mirror, adjusted my hair a little bit. I looked stunning, even with my baby bump.

Saul was very emotional that morning, he had checked on me a couple of times, making sure I was okay. I had not seen Marcus that much in the last twenty-four hours, he did not bother me with calls. I was at Saul's and he knew the care I was being given between Rick and Margaret. Besides, he was just as busy as I was.

Rick had prepared a Maybach S600 Pullman. It was my first time seeing that beauty. I checked in with my bridesmaids and my junior bridesmaids, who dressed similarly to each other in chiffon. My two flower girls were also in chiffon dresses, but one had a white satin bodice. The color of all the dresses was a dusty pink. Just enough color to compliment my own dress. We arrived at the cathedral a few minutes past eleven that morning and everyone was already waiting. There was not anything extra in the decoration of the cathedral. It was laid with red rugs from the entrance to the alter. Lightening made for a soft and romantic atmosphere. Families and friends were seated in rows and I could see workers from the firm cheering at my arrival.

I was the reason for the day; every eye was on me as much as they were on Marcus. He was dressed in a black tuxedo with tails, some black leather shoes, which I am sure was made by his favorite shoe brand, Mazlan. His hair was so curly and long that looked like he was in his teens. I smiled with all the joy in the world; I wondered how a nobody girl like me could find herself a charming prince such as Marcus. I would never dream of a wedding like this, even as a kid. Saul cupped my hands in his, almost teary as he walked me to the alter, while the flower girls continued to usher us in with pink and light blue rose petals. I could not hold back the tears. There were signs of joy everywhere and it made me happy. For the first time in the six months, I totally was oblivious to my bulging belly.

Now, I was standing face to face with Marcus; Saul had taken his place beside Margaret, who was sitting alongside the Mathew's. The Bishop looked at us as we continued to smile, while I stared at him from the light blue lace veil that covered my head and face down to my shoulder. He asked, "Marcus Mathew, do you take Samantha Amanda Weinstein as your lawfully wedded wife, to love and to cherish till death do you part?"

Marcus stared into my eyes, smiled, and said, "Yes, till death do us part."

I also said my vows and accepted to be the wife of Marcus Mathew. The Bishop eventually said, "You may now kiss the bride." Marcus lifted the veil gently; with all the happiness he could have.

He was all smiles, like someone who had just won a trophy. He kissed me ever so passionately; I felt the babies in my tummy move – it was blissful. After the rites, vows, and all programs had finished; we were led outside the cathedral. There was the snapping of pictures and exchange of gestures and wishes. After photos were taken, Mike opened the door to a black Maserati that was supposed to take me and Marcus to the reception. I was seeing it for the first time ever, he bought it especially for this today. Marcus continued to hold my hands the whole time, making certain I was extremely comfortable with the entire day. And I was, I was thrilled.

Our arrival at the reception was grand; we were met by most of New York's high society, with smiles and wishes on their faces. The reception décor had a luxurious touch to everything; Rick had done a wonderful job. The entire venue covered in shades of pink flowers, on the floor and floating in the air. The middle of the dining area had a drop ring light, supplying the whole place with ambiance, while making sure that the center stage was the focus. It was where I took to the dance floor with my father, then with my husband. There were several dignitaries, men of wealth, and a host of others. The male attendants were dressed in a contemporary tuxedo with a solid coat, vest that was gray, and striped pants. Several local papers and gossip magazines had contacted the Matthew's publicist to try and get as much detail as they could. Saul had spent half a million dollars on the wedding, and I must say Rick had been sensible about it. From my wedding gown to my shoes, he had made the right choices. And even though I had been standing on low heels, I was perfectly aware of my body and its needs. Moreover, my babies were enjoying the moment as well, except for one or two mood swings caused by tiredness, the day was perfect.

The Matthew's family had driven in limos as well and every prominent person was in attendance. Marcus had mentioned later that his family had spent close to a hundred thousand dollars on the wedding. Saul had pledged his commitment to making me happy and was ever so delighted to sign the checks. The Mathew's seemed to never run out of cash. It was a glamorous societal wedding, to say the least. However, the last person I was expecting to see was Kenneth. How he made it to the event, I could never know. He was there with some lady who must have fallen among the invitees to the reception. He smiled and waved at me as I caught a glimpse of him sitting in the crowd of honorable people and guests. I made sure to scan the building, looking for Joseph. Not that I was expecting him, but I knew that there was no way he could ignore the publicity of the lawyer who caught John Marcus Matthew Jr, one of the most eligible bachelors in New York.

Moments later, the head of ceremony invited Adele to the stage. She was prompt as; she had arrived at the Mathew's a day earlier. Marcus adores her and her music. I would not deny that she sings songs that helps a drowning soul, as well as lifts the spirit with her loving and joyful songs.

Marcus and I danced effortlessly. I rested my head on his shoulder as he held me close, making sure to help me keep my balance as Adele sang some of her sweetest love songs. Elton also later dedicated one of his well-crafted songs to us. The celebration continued. People were merry as the entertainment of the event passed on to a band after the guest artists were done entertaining us.

I had danced with John Mathew, Sr and I was in the arms of Saul when I started feeling tired. However, I managed to dance with my dad, it was a joyful one. We laughed hysterically at his jokes and teasing, he even showed off his moves on the dance floor. About a minute or two into Marcus's arms, he noticed I was fatigued. "Sam, you do not look well; your beautiful face has lost its color. I think you should sit down, or better yet, let us leave. Rick can handle everything from here on." he said, planting kisses on my lips.

"Yes honey, I'm a little tired, and the babies seem to be dancing…" I said to keep the worry from his face. "But I think we should stay for my dad and your father's toast. Perhaps water will help for now." I furthered, as he placed his hands on my belly, gently rubbing it. We were still swinging from left to right as Marcus continued to rub my tummy in the middle of the dance floor, some folks were watching, and I could see them smiling.

"Sweetheart, just our dad's toast, then we go home, and I will rub those pretty little feet of yours," Marcus replied. After that statement, I felt the room spinning. The next thing felt was dizzy and I quietly rested my head on Marcus' shoulders. He picked me up at once, as a groom would pick up his bride. He did not want to alarm the audience, so he signaled at Mike while he whispered to me, "Sam, raise your hands." I understood what he was trying to do, so I raised one of my full arms up, and everyone cheered with clapping and laughter. Marcus carried me from the dance floor as Mike ran out to prepare the limousine. I was conscious of what was happening; however, I was not sure I could move a limb any longer. Mike had the limo parked just around the corner for us to get into quickly, only Rick had followed Marcus as he carried me to the car. I once again summoned all my energy and managed to wave goodbye while my husband helped me into the car, and the security team led the way to the hospital.

The moment I was placed in the limousine, I went blank.

Mike had put a call through to Dr. McCullough. On arrival at the street that led to the hospital, about a few blocks away, I regained consciousness and told Marcus I had sharp pains that felt cramp-like. He looked at his watch and said, "tell me when the next one happens." About 10 minutes later, another increasing pain happened at the same time we reached the hospital. Two of the hospital staff were waiting with a bed. The attending nurse placed her hand on my belly, apparently trying to check the position of the babies. She rubbed her hand over my belly, slipped her hands into my vagina, and said, "Mrs. Matthew, you are in labor, and it appears that your babies are coming fast." I checked around for Marcus, and he was right beside me, fidgeting while I squeezed my face in pain. He did not say a word.

My heavy body laid on the bed helplessly, while Dr. McCullough did a quick pelvic examination and said, "there is no time, get her into delivery and prep her." Marcus got into action with the nurse's aide and got himself into a gown. Everything was happening so fast, and the pain was unbearable. I felt breathless, like I was having a panic attack. Dr. McCullough said, "Give her a shot to calm her anxiety and help with the pain."

The doctor asked me to push with all my strength. Marcus held my hands and said, "Baby, please push for us!" and I did. I pushed and pushed until Dr. McCullough looked over to Marcus and said, "Mr. Mathew, one of the babies are coming." The nurse beside the doctor held on to a stainless-steel plate which had all these various instruments inside. The doctor said to her, "get ready to cut the cord, the babies are on their way."

No one had time to say anything except to obey orders. Marcus held on to my hand and continued to inspire me to push. The first baby eventually came, and the doctor helped Marcus cut the cord and hand him to the nurse, while the second baby was crowning. I was in excruciating pain. I did not have to struggle that much with the second baby, I summoned my last ounce of courage held on to Marcus like I was holding on to a lifeline and pushed. As soon as my second baby boy came out, and I heard my first-born cry, I passed out.

I came back to reality a few hours later; the babies placed in bed the beside me. The nurse helped them to my chest, and I had my first pictures with my bundles of joy. Marcus had taken pictures of us, including himself, with his smartphone. He said they were just about a few minutes apart, and they looked like their father.

The following day, I was still at the hospital and Marcus was right there with me. He had made sure I was cared for. His head of security, Mike, not anyone else, would be in the corridor, waiting. Later that day, we received both grandparents at the hospital. Saul filled with life as much as John was. I was showered with kisses. Something I had never known when I was born.

After about twelve hours at the hospital, I was feeling a lot better. Marcus came to my room and asked, "are you good?"

I responded, "Yes, Mr. Mathew."

He helped me up and we were on our way to see our sons, when Dr. Wright, the boy's pediatrician, met us in the hallway to the private nursery. "Mr. and Mrs. Matthew, it would seem the smallest of the boys is suffering from serve jaundice."

"What does that mean?" I asked.

"Sometimes it just happens, but usually it is when some of the mother's blood passes over in the womb, from incompatible blood types."

The thoughts of joy that filled my heart suddenly burst into a rain cloud. Dr. Wright said, "I have him under light therapy and oxygen. He is two pounds smaller than his brother, who is healthy and shows no jaundice."

"Marcus, I cannot lose him, please help our son." I cried.

"Dr. Wright tell me what needs to be done at once. We will not lose our son." You could see on Marcus's face that he would will our son to live.

"Nurse!" he shouted, "send the family home."

"Mike," he called, "I need you here to take Samantha back to her room." He began barking orders like I had never heard or seen him do before.

"Marcus, you need to see this," he said.

"What Mike?" Marcus said, "What is that and why is it important? My son's life is at stake!" Mike handed Marcus a white letter that seemed like a formal one. "It's from the court," he said.

The moment I heard *court* I looked at Marcus. He was staring at me with a skeptical look. My heart skipped a beat when he went through it and said, "It is from Joseph's attorney. I will deal with him later. Fuck him and his attorney!" He shouted.

www.ingramcontent.com/pod-product-compliance
Lightning Source LLC
Chambersburg PA
CBHW071840190726
48292CB00005B/1851